Partita

A Psychological Mystery

Madeleine Herrmann

Edited by Cinny Green

Plain View Press
P. O. 42255
Austin, TX 78704

plainviewpress.net
sb@plainviewpress.net
512-441-2452

Copyright Madeleine Herrmann, 2009. All rights reserved.
ISBN: 978-1-891386-94-7
Library of Congress Number: 2009925697

Disclaimer: This is a work of fiction. Any resemblances to real people and events are coincidental.

Cover design by Susan Bright

Acknowledgments

I acknowledge and thank all of the people who have been part of my life. The parents and relatives who helped me grow up and wade through difficult episodes with faith and love, the lovers who challenged the state of my consciousness and helped me mature further, my children through whom I learned to be a mother, all the friends who serendipitously appeared at the right time and helped shape my vision of humanity. They are too numerous to name. They know who they are. Thank you all. You are part of who I am now.

Recently I have been helped by all the friends who read my story and encouraged me to pursue its telling, and all the members of the No Coast Writers group, especially Susan Mihalic and then Kyra Ryan, who edited part of the story. I also thank Ellen Kleiner of Blessingway Author Services, my partner and loving supporter Thomas French, and last but not least, my wonderful writing coach, Cinny Green, who was able to understand the depth of it all as she worked with me on delicate interpretations of the characters' actions.

This story is dedicated to the memory of my husband, Friedrich Wolfgang Herrmann, who died tragically in February 1969. It is also dedicated to our four children: Richard, Erika, Steven, and Caroline, who manifest his creative spirit through their thoughtful writing, poetry, music, photography, and drawing. Fred always gave us an appreciation for beauty and love of the artistic pursuit in spite of his difficult times.

Thank you, Fred, for all these gifts. May your bright spirit keep shining through our lives.

A Betty
nes meilleurs
avec
voeuy
madile —

On a single staff, for a little instrument, the man writes a whole world of the deepest thoughts and most powerful feelings. If I could picture myself writing, or even conceiving, such a piece, I am certain the extreme excitement and emotional tension would have driven me mad.

—Johannes Brahms
In a letter to Clara Schumann about the Ciaccona, the fifth movement of Bach's Partita II in D minor (1877)

Contents

Allemanda

The Dark Dance

Ernst was too afraid to move. The room was bathed in gray light as his wife Manou rose to wake the children. In a hollow voice emerging heavily from his throat, he said, "I'm sick today."

Manou winced and asked, "You sound strange, Ernst. Are you feverish?" She ran a hand across his forehead. "Perhaps you have the flu."

He moved his head away because his skin felt too thin to bear her touch and her concern. He looked out the window at Mount Diablo, shrouded with fog in the distance. The sight of it enveloped in a blanket of mist seemed serene compared to the bedroom, which caged rather than comforted him. He and Manou had lived in California a long time, but this house in Walnut Creek had never felt like home. It didn't embrace him like the home they had built in Pleasant Hill. If she hadn't made them move, maybe things would have been different, he thought.

When he looked back into the room, she was standing at the foot of the bed, her body under the cotton nightgown still athletic after bearing four children. Despite standing so close, to him she seemed very far away, and he wasn't sure how long she had been hovering there. Time slipped away from him so often now that it could have been a second or an hour. He finally remembered her question and mumbled, "I don't have a fever, but yes, that's it, I probably have the flu."

"You want me to bring you some tea?" she asked.

"No. It will go away," he replied, emotionless.

Manou gazed questioningly at him a moment longer with her sharp brown eyes, then, looking at the clock, exclaimed, "*Mon Dieu.* It's seven o'clock already! I'm going to be late." She threw on her robe and left the room so quickly that her departure created a current of energy that made Ernst dizzy.

Ernst looked toward the window again. Outside, the goat-man stood in the rain, the mountain behind him like a cloak. At once his redeemer and his nemesis, the fetid human-beast came more often now, each time asking Ernst, in a guttural, mysteriously accented voice, "Have you practiced? Are you ready?" His question was the same one his mother, Mutti, had asked day after day about his violin playing when he had been a boy. But this cloven-footed master, Ernst knew, wanted something different. Ernst had practiced for months, but no longer the violin. Never again the violin. His fear evaporated for the moment. He looked straight into the goat-man's small jaundiced eyes with resignation and acceptance.

Manou's voice from downstairs jolted Ernst's attention away from the apparition. She was hustling their four children through their morning routine before school. She taught high school French classes and had to arrive at school early, so her impatience was thinly veiled. "Florence, eat up. Sophia, toss your nightgown in the hamper. Don't forget your report, Karl."

All of you go, so I can end this, Ernst thought. Then he muttered out loud to the goat-man, "You are the only one who knows how much I need to rest. I won't fail this time." His own voice sounded hollow to him, like it was coming from a cavern beneath the sea. He knew that when Manou had winced earlier, it was because she had heard the hollowness, too, and was puzzled by it but also irritated. Manou had tried so many times to break through the wall of isolation surrounding him—with love, patience, and even justifiable anger at his distance, his blaming, and his drinking. But although he had tried in the past, Ernst could no longer escape the clutches of the yellow-eyed, cloven-footed being that enticed him. He had lost any will to resist following the goat-man, who now drank with him, swam with him, bathed with him, and walked with him in the winter rain, teaching Ernst how to go under his loss, under the façade of his meaningless daily life, under the very air he breathed, into water.

As his wife hurried back into the bedroom to dress, Ernst saw lines of tension around her mouth, making her look sad, and for a moment he felt sorry for Manou. But instantly, a wave of contempt swept over him, replacing the compassion. Marie Madeleine, he thought as he had many times, is her real name. The French version of Mary Magdalene. Was Mary Magdalene the best friend of Jesus or the prostitute from whom emerged the seven devils, the seven deadly vices? He clenched his fists under the covers as resentment against Manou engulfed him. Oh, yes, lust, pride, and covetousness certainly applied to Manou's attitudes. Whore at her core, lust and pride had motivated her since the day he had met her. She lusted after this extravagant house, not because it had more space and was closer to better schools, as she claimed, but out of insatiable greed. This American way is so gluttonous. I would have to work forever when all I ever wanted was simply to play my violin. What's more, she has had her success at the expense of mine. She had to go back to school, had to teach, had to sabotage my superior ability and intelligence. Mary Magdalene was not redeemed by her love for Jesus, for in her manifestation as Manou, she has unleashed a demon upon me. He heard the rasping sadistic chuckle of the goat-man affirming his thoughts.

Down the hall, Karl and Francis squabbled. Manou said, "Ernst, could you see what's...?" but she interrupted her request with an exasperated sigh and rushed from her dressing table to sort out their problem. Ernst looked back at his specter. He was frowning impatiently. Everyone's impatient with me, Ernst thought. Mutti, Manou, my children, my students, and even the goat-man who has waited so patiently over the years. It is time to act.

Today he would do what the goat-man had trained him to do, he told himself, feeling a mysterious combination of anxiety and anticipation. As Manou returned again to finish dressing, Ernst propped a textbook on his chest to hide his anxious eyes but peered over the top to watch her. She pulled on a sweater and wool skirt, applied her makeup, and clasped her luxuriant black hair away from her forehead with a small tortoiseshell clip. So chic. So French. Then she took a step toward the bed but stopped, crossed her arms over her chest, and pleaded, "Ernst? What *is* the matter?"

Ernst answered in his hollow, distant voice, "Nothing."

He had never told her about the goat-man. What did it matter? She was unable to understand anything he did now that she was so focused on her own interests. In fact, only once had he tried to show the goat-man to anyone. He had been driving home along a winding road from Bodega Bay after an outing alone with the children and told them they would see something special, not human, on the mountain. As the fading light illuminated the western slope, Ernst saw his cloven-footed redeemer watching them from a crag. Pointing, Ernst exclaimed, "Look quickly! Do you see the creature up there near the top, with legs and hooves like a goat? Look, look now," he exclaimed. Francis and Florence, the two youngest, seemed almost persuaded. Florence answered, "Oh, yes, Dad, I see it, I think. Near the pine tree?"

Twelve-year-old Sophia said, "Come on, Dad. There's nothing there."

Karl was thirteen and scoffed in his new low voice, "There are only a thousand pine trees up there."

Of course, they couldn't see the goat-man, and they laughed at such a preposterous idea, Ernst thought bitterly. Laughed at me. Someday they'll remember it, though, and I'll be the one who laughs.

Manou leaned over and kissed his forehead. He smelled the salt of her skin and the musky French perfume her mother gave her every birthday. Manou always had the power to intoxicate him, and now her seductiveness briefly awakened him, making him want to escape from the goat-man. He strained inwardly to reach for her, but his arms felt like dead weights. Of course, he couldn't reach for Marie Madeleine. She was never more than lust, he reminded himself.

Manou watched him for a minute, smiled tenderly, then dropped her arms, and said, "Well, I'll call between classes to see how you're doing."

Instead of saying good-bye, Ernst propped the book closer to his face. After Manou had left the room, he let it thump back down on his chest and reached for his latest lifeline: his flicker light, a tool used to induce hypnosis, meant to relax his mind, help him sleep, and—he secretly hoped—soothe his inner torment. His colleagues in the psychology department at the university had sworn that flicker fusion was the mental health breakthrough of the sixties, and Ernst participated in a study of its hypnotic effectiveness. He claimed he intended to apply hypnosis to the teaching of foreign languages, to ease students' inhibitions. Or so he told the professors who thought him extraordinary because he offered many insights that helped guide their research. Unknown to them, he used the hypnotic device at home, to calm himself by staring at the pulsing light. But it had not helped. It was too late.

Ernst heard the goat-man flick his long coiled fingernails on the windowpane, with his hairy human-like hand. His tapping was demanding, turning Ernst's attention away from the soothing flicker light to the beast's steady yellow eyes.

The children called out their good-byes from downstairs as they gathered their schoolbooks and lunches.

"Dad?"

"We're going."

"Bye, Dad."

Ensnared in the goat-man's stare, Ernst's couldn't reply.

He heard disappointed murmurs, then from Manou: "Never mind. Your dad probably fell back asleep. Come on, everyone in the car."

The engine started in the driveway, and they drove away through the rain, leaving him in torment.

"Think about the peace you will feel," rasped the goat-man. "You just need to do what I have asked. It is simple, so simple." The goat-man laughed and his grotesque red tongue lurched from his mouth.

Ernst jammed his eyes closed, turned back toward the calming blinking light, desperately staring at it from behind his closed eyelids. Then he summoned his favorite music, Bach's Partita II in D minor, from deep within him. Ah, there I am: Ernst Feidler, the virtuoso violinist. The melody warmed his whole body like a swirling bath, the first movement, the Allemanda, a deceptively simple, deeply sad, dark dance. Ernst wept as he hummed softly.

Ernst heard the goat-man snicker through his long, thick nose, and abruptly the melody disappeared. He felt cold, and his inner world shifted as he realized that he was no virtuoso but merely a fiddler. Ernst huddled under the blankets and thought, all my life, I dreamed of being an exceptional violinist, but no, instead I became a language professor, a mere plebian. I sabotaged my own success as a musician.

The goat-man held out his hands, enticing Ernst with a fearsome friendliness. Huge raindrops sprayed around the specter in slow motion, and water overflowed his palms cupped like chalices. The goat-man smiled. Whether it was an invitation or command, Ernst knew that the goat-man was calling him to the communion of water.

♫

After her two morning French classes, Manou went to call Ernst in the empty teacher's lounge. A gale was blowing outside, bringing with it a heavy rain that rattled like marbles on the school's metal roof. At first, the number was busy. On her second try, he picked up. "How are you doing?" she shouted into the phone to be heard above the clatter.

"Okay...I'm doing okay," Ernst answered in a muffled voice as if he were mumbling in a dream or speaking through a soft cloth.

"Who called?"

"I was just talking to Dimitri. He's going to watch my classes."

"That's good. I'm glad you're staying home. The weather is terrible, so typical of February. Keep warm," Manou advised.

There was no answer. Manou searched for him through the silence. "I wish I could be in bed, too...with you."

"Yes," he whispered faintly, like a voice disappearing in a fog.

She said a little louder, "I'll be home after my last class. I'll pick up the kids and bring something good for dinner."

"You ought to get back to class," Ernst ordered, suddenly clear and dismissive in a familiar cranky tone. "Good-bye."

"Okay. Bye." Manou hung up, reassured that he was just a little sick and irritable. After all, she was used to his periodic moodiness and unresponsiveness, and they really hadn't communicated that much in a long time. She was less and less interested in opening new channels when he seemed unwilling to meet her halfway. I worry too much, she told herself as she glanced in the teacher's room mirror. Then she quickly brushed her hair and returned to class.

During her afternoon French class, the intercom in the classroom abruptly buzzed, interrupting her explanation of uses of the subjunctive tense. "Yes?" she answered.

"Mrs. Feidler, please come to Principal Thomson's office right away. It's urgent," said the secretary.

"Is it about my children?"

"Just come now. Please." The secretary added, "We'll send a monitor."

"All right. I'll be there in about five minutes." She turned to the class. "I guess you all get a little break today. Stay here and finish the exercises on page seventy-two. I'm sure they'll send someone in a minute."

She stuffed her students' homework in her satchel and hurried down the linoleum halls, through the blue door with the sign that read CONTRA COSTA HIGH SCHOOL in bold red letters with a cartoon of a red devil, their sports mascot, below the words. Inside the office, the secretary was talking on the phone. Manou nervously pushed open the principal's door and saw two men in front of Principal Thomson's desk. "Please, come in and sit down, Mrs. Feidler," said the principal. "This is Inspector Kravitz and Inspector Carlson from the city police department." She looked at the two men, both holding wet raincoats across their arms. One was about forty, jowly and balding, dressed in a wrinkled gray suit. The other, a younger man, wore a navy blue blazer with wide lapels and a white golf shirt with a coffee stain on the front.

Inspector Kravitz cleared his throat while Carlson pulled a notebook from his blazer pocket and reported, "Dr. Feidler called the city police this morning at 10:23. He said—and I quote from the dispatcher's log— 'My wife is suicidal. She might hurt the children. Please check on her. Hurry!' then he gave this location and hung up."

Perplexed, Manou realized that Ernst had called them shortly after her phone call to him from the teacher's lounge, just a couple of hours ago. What could he have been thinking? She jumped up and asserted, "I am *not* suicidal. I've been in class all morning. Ernst wasn't feeling well when I left the house...he had the flu or something." Her heart thudded in her chest. "Please...tell me what you think is going on."

Inspector Kravitz took her by the elbow, gently eased her back in her chair, and continued, "We're not sure. We checked the house, and he's not there." He exchanged a look with Carlson.

Inspector Carlson consulted his notebook again, and then reported, "At exactly 12:13 p.m., a psychiatrist—a Dr. James Campbell from Kaiser Hospital—called, reporting that Dr. Ernst Feidler had come to the emergency room seeking medication for anxiety. After examining the patient, Dr. Campbell thought he should drive immediately to a psychiatric clinic for observation. Dr. Feidler consented, but when the

14

doctor went to make the arrangements, Dr. Feidler left the hospital. The physician was concerned that Dr. Feidler is in a dangerous frame of mind."

"That's absurd. My husband isn't dangerous and would not harm anyone. He has a doctorate in psychology himself." She felt her voice get shrill, so she took a deep breath, trying to maintain her composure, even in this maddening circumstance.

"Could you tell me what you've been doing this morning, Mrs. Feidler?" Inspector Kravitz asked, looking at her with expressionless hazel eyes.

"When I left my husband this morning, he was in bed reading. I dropped off the kids at their schools and came here, just as I do every day. I called him about ten—after my second class. Ernst sounded okay. Are you sure he said that *I* was suicidal? I don't understand."

Inspector Carlson stated, "The psychiatrist at Kaiser was concerned that Dr. Feidler might be having a nervous breakdown, since he was experiencing a hallucination about a goat. Would you know anything about that, ma'am?"

Manou struggled to put together the hollow sound of Ernst's voice and the distant look in his eyes that morning with this bizarre diagnosis of a nervous breakdown. Across from her, Principal Thomson was sweating. He was a local guy good at fire drills and curriculum meetings, but he normally farmed out staff problems to the guidance counselor. Cops, suicide, and nervous breakdowns were definitely over his head. Her familiar disdain for soft Americans surfaced. She had never met one who could truly comprehend the horrors she and Ernst had experienced separately as children during the World War II. They had both crouched in dark bomb shelters during air raids; walked in streets littered with shrapnel, debris, and crushed bodies; and lived in constant fear of what would happen next. Although he was German and she French, they had shared the ability to endure through troubled times. So how could Ernst be falling apart now?

Inspector Kravitz asked, "Does your husband have any weapons?"

Hesitantly, Manou answered, "Yes, he has a hunting rifle, but he hasn't hunted in years."

"Do you know where it is?"

"In the bedroom closet. It's never loaded because of the children."

The inspectors immediately put on their damp raincoats and ordered Manou, "You have to come along with us. We'll stop at your house to check if the gun is there, then we'll pick your kids up from school."

Principal Thomson wiped his forehead with a handkerchief and looked immensely relieved. "I'll find a substitute, Mrs. Feidler, so don't worry."

Inspector Kravitz said, a little more softly, "You should stay with someone until we sort this out. Do you have family in the area?"

"I have no family in California."

He stopped at the office door and looked puzzled. "No one? Why not?"

"They are all in France. Ernst's mother is in Germany."

"And why do they live in Europe?" His question sounded like an accusation.

She frowned. "Because they are Europeans."

"Oh yes, of course," Kravitz said as he wrote in his little notebook. "And are you a citizen of the United States?"

"I've lived here seventeen years. Ernst served in the American military. We became citizens more than a decade ago."

"We have to check, I hope you understand. In the meantime, you and your children should have some company."

Manou tried to think about where to go until this peculiar mystery about Ernst was solved. They both knew so many people, but as a tight family, they didn't really have many intimate friends. She knew several women outside of work, but normally they just chatted about life with kids—except her skiing buddy Lucy who had lost her husband to cancer a few years ago and called Manou many times to talk about her grief. Having experienced all kinds of suffering during the war, Manou had been able to give Lucy useful advice about coping. Lucy had told her to call anytime so she could reciprocate Manou's support.

"Lucy Carter on Mimosa Lane is my friend," Manou told Kravitz.

"You can call her from your house."

Curious students stared from classroom doors as the detectives led Manou out of the school. She breathed a sigh of relief that Karl had classes in another part of the building. Outside, the inspectors led her to their unmarked gray police van. As they drove her home, Manou was filled with a fear as ill defined as the gray van moving slowly through the dreary rain.

The red truck was not in the driveway. With a policeman on either side of her, she opened the front door of the house and called for Ernst, but there was no answer. Inspector Carlson went up to the bedroom with her. The bed was unmade but empty. The window was open and rain had soaked the carpet. Manou shut and locked the window while the detective checked the closet, where he found the dusty gun behind the soft shadows of their clothes. Carlson tagged it and took it to the van, while Manou quickly called Lucy and explained the strange situation. Lucy told her to bring the children right over. They returned to Contra Costa High School to get Karl and then to the junior high for Sophia and Francis. By the time they picked up Florence at the elementary school, their anxious breaths fogged up the windows in the van. Manou had a hard time explaining the situation to them or even understanding it herself. They each asked, "Dad's missing? Will he be okay?"

She hugged them and could only answer, "I'm sure he will be. We just have to wait at Lucy's and see what happens." Florence drew a big question mark in the mist on the car window.

The police dropped them off at Lucy's, where the children drank hot chocolate and ate cookies in silence while Manou wrapped her hands around her cup of tea to keep them from trembling. Later, after the children had curled up together in blankets like a row of identical spoons on the living room floor, Lucy hugged Manou and helped her upstairs to a dark bedroom. As she lay in bed trying to sleep, Manou felt lost. "Ernst, where are you?" she asked over and over, like a chant, until the doorbell rang at 10:00 p.m. Manou leapt out of bed and ran downstairs, where Lucy was letting a young uniformed officer into the hall and the children stood wide-eyed in their rumpled school clothes.

"Mrs. Feidler?" asked the officer, nervously turning his cap in his hands.

"Yes. My husband? Did you find him?"

"Yes, ma'am, we did." The officer looked down.

"For God's sake, officer, where is he?" Manou asked impatiently.

"He was found in Danville Creek off Highway 680 just north of the Alamo exit . . . Are you sure you want the children to hear this, ma'am?"

"Just tell us!" she demanded.

"I'm sorry to report that he drowned, Mrs. Feidler...under his truck. He is...deceased."

"Daddy!" Sophia shrieked from somewhere deep in her body. Her head and shoulders crumbled downward, and in the next instant, her hands, like claws, began tearing her clothes, first slowly, then frantically. Ripping her shirt open, the buttons flying out in all directions, she began to scrape at her chest as if trying to shed her skin. Lucy wrapped her arms around the girl to keep her from hurting herself. Florence and Karl sat down heavily on the sofa and stared at the hysterical Sophia. Francis slumped next to them, sobbing into Karl's sleeve.

Manou stepped toward her children to comfort them, but felt as though she were stepping into a dark cloud, and fainted. When she regained consciousness back in Lucy's guest bedroom, with immense relief she thought she had been dreaming, but after hearing sobbing downstairs, the raw truth came flooding back: the police, the rush from school, the distraught children, Ernst dead, drowned under his truck.

Manou slowly descended the carpeted stairs to where Lucy was comforting the two littlest children, whose faces were swollen from crying. Karl gazed blankly in shock. Sophia was wrapped in Lucy's bathrobe. Manou gasped, "I'm sorry,"—an apology that embraced Ernst's incomprehensible death as well as her own collapse when they needed her. The children leaned into her and wrapped themselves around her body. Fourteen-year-old Karl asked, "What are we going to do now, Mom?"

Lucy answered the immediate question as she announced, "You all are going to go home to your own beds now. You'll feel better there. I'll drive you to school now to get your car, Manou." Lucy began bundling the kids back in their jackets while Manou stood in a daze.

"Manou, after the officer carried you to the guestroom, I had him call Dr. Tremont," Lucy explained. "The doctor will meet you at your house in about thirty minutes. He told us you all should go home."

Manou could only nod and take the youngest by their hands and lead them to Lucy's station wagon in the driveway.

When they arrived a half-hour later, Doctor Tremont was waiting on the porch. His compassion and calm authority settled the children, who had known him for many years. He gave them all small doses of Valium so they could sleep; Manou said she would take hers later when she was sure they were all resting, and she tucked her two pills in her sweater pocket. Lucy and the doctor were hesitant to leave after the children were in bed, but Manou insisted, telling them, "I just need to face this alone, you know."

Dr. Tremont said, "Call me tomorrow. I have something important to talk to you about."

"I will," she agreed, and they left Manou with the devastating reality of her aloneness in the house she had shared with her husband of sixteen years.

Like a prowler, she entered the bedroom Ernst had been in that morning. The flicker light was still blinking on the bedside table. I wonder why I didn't notice it when I came here with the inspector this afternoon, she thought listlessly. She switched it off and wandered around, searching within these walls for his scent, his presence, and some explanation for what had happened to him. She looked on top of his bureau and saw his driver's license, his credit card, and some money. She glanced down at the rumpled bed and, in her desperation, whipped off all the covers and threw the pillows against the wall. She picked up the book he had been reading when she left and thumbed through the pages. Did the fact that it was a book about hypnosis provide a clue? The words swam as she tried to read the dry, scientific text. Had he been trying to hypnotize himself and thus had the accident? Was there an answer anywhere in the minutiae of this room? She slammed the book down and opened the drawer in his bedside table but again found nothing—not even a bottle of pills or a notebook of last-minute scribbling. "Nothing" had been his only haunting answer to her concern that morning. Nothing! She dropped to her knees against the bed, gasping as if she had been struck in the chest.

None of it made sense. How could this man drown? He had been physically fit his whole life—a tireless swimmer, an athlete, a builder, a hiker. He was also so intelligent, a professor and linguist who spoke five languages fluently, and had even started a new career as a psychologist. They were always moving forward; that's what she and Ernst did in life. The man she loved was dead, and suddenly the memory of his face, with its glorious smile and penetrating blue eyes, seemed like a mask, while his true self remained hidden.

Manou crouched on the floor of the bedroom, utterly alone now. She pulled the two Valiums from her sweater pocket, jammed them in her mouth, and swallowed them without water. She closed her fists; clenching her teeth, she wrapped her arms around herself like an armor, shielding herself against her fear and, mostly, the flood of emotions threatening to break her apart. She stood up and started to run out of the room, stopped abruptly, and began to sway, slowly, in a dark dance. She could hear the music, as rich and resonant as if he were playing it now in this empty room. She swayed until her body collapsed on the bed, still clothed, and she fell into a dreamless vortex of sleep.

Manou was up at dawn. While the children slept, she got dressed and absently went through the morning rituals of making coffee and toast. In numb shock, she listened to the news of Ernst's death on the radio, hearing the details the police had gathered overnight about the accident. According to witnesses, the red truck had swerved off Highway 680, careened down an embankment into a canal, and plunged into water that came up to the window but no further. The truck had no visible damage. A witness said he could not see anyone in the cab of the truck as it veered off the road. When the police arrived at the scene of the accident, the driver's window was open but the doors remained closed. Ernst wasn't found until the police hauled the pickup out of the water and his waterlogged body rose to the surface from under the vehicle.

A thump against the front door signaled the arrival of the morning newspaper. Manou fetched it from the porch and saw that on the front page was a picture of the truck, half submerged in the water, behind which stood men in ponchos and high rubber boots. The article repeated the details she had heard on the radio and then gave a biography of the man who had been her husband: a German who had made his life in America, a soldier and a linguist at the Army Language School, an accomplished professor of languages at Valley College, a researcher working on a brilliant electronics project to help reproduce the sounds of foreign languages, a violinist, a genius who succeeded at everything he tried. Apart from the details of Ernst's life, Manou was surprised that the reporter mentioned his fatigue and stress. Who told them that? The writer posed the question: Was it an accidental drowning or a suicide? *Suicide?* Her mind circled the thought like a bird afraid to land on an unfamiliar branch. She asked an absent Ernst for answers: What happened, Ernst? What was going on in your mind? Where were you headed on Highway 680? How did you end up at the creek and lose control of the truck in the rain? A genius has many reasons to be stressed, but you coped, even if you had become more remote lately and drank too much.

Manou desperately wanted to piece together the enigma of Ernst's death and understand his motivations, especially if he had indeed committed suicide—no, that was unthinkable. She made some calls, and slowly mapped the various events of Ernst's last day: After she had left for school, Ernst had called Dimitri Komarov from the language department, *not* to get him to cover his classes—as Ernst had told her on the phone—but to reveal that he was suffering from anxiety, was afraid to face his students, and could not teach. This was incredible to Manou. Ernst had been reluctant to discuss personal problems with her, much less a colleague.

"Ernst wanted to talk but," Dimitri told Manou, "I didn't feel like I could help. He was really upset so I told him to go see a doctor."

He said this so apologetically that Manou felt the need to comfort him. "It's all right, Dimitri, that was the right thing to do." She knew that Ernst had called the police right after that with the lie about her being suicidal. This still made no sense.

Next, Ernst took Dimitri's advice and had called Dr. Tremont. "Thanks for calling, Manou. This is what I wanted to talk to you about," said the kind family physician. "I had a full schedule and couldn't fit him in. I told him to immediately go to Kaiser Hospital and see the emergency room psychiatrist." Manou heard the same apologetic, almost guilty tone of the second person who had been unable to help her husband.

Yet, again, Ernst had listened and had driven to Kaiser to see a psychiatrist in the emergency room. When Manou called, Dr. Campbell came to the phone and said, "I grasped the severity of Ernst's anxiety and advised him to go immediately to the mental health hospital in Martinez, which has state-of-the-art facilities and diagnostics." However, Ernst had left while the psychiatrist was processing the referral. And the doctor had called the police. Manou could hear him turning the pages of his report. "I was also worried about what I felt was Ernst's dangerous state of mind. He was having hallucinations."

"If he was in a dangerous state of mind, what made you think he could drive himself to Martinez?"

The psychiatrist paused. "If you have any other questions, please call the hospital attorney."

Bastard, thought Manou. All he cares about is a malpractice suit because his patient died. I would never do such a thing as sue. All I care about is the truth.

Then Ernst apparently left the hospital, drove down the highway, not to Martinez, but south until he veered off 680 in the rain, lost control, slid into the canal, and drowned.

The phone rang and Manou hesitated to pick it up. The prospect of more unexpected news made her stomach clench. Nothing worse could happen, she told herself. Don't be foolish. She picked up the receiver. It was Florence's friend Cindy. "Can I talk to her?" she asked. "I feel so bad about your dad...I mean, her dad. Oh, you know."

"Thank you, Cindy, I know what you mean. I'll have her call you when she gets up."

Manou sat back and tried to shake the tension out of her arms and shoulders, but it didn't help. She still felt like she had a wire net holding her together. She had all the pieces of the puzzle except perhaps the most mysterious and troubling one—the reason for his breakdown and if it had caused an accident or driven him to suicide. Did he break down because she pushed him too hard to move to Walnut Creek?

He often said he hated it.

Had she not paid enough attention to his work and the slow loss of his possibilities for a career in music as his other work consumed his time?

He stopped playing the violin long ago. It was his choice.

Had his breakdown been caused by his mother's endless expectations for his success?

She had lived with them on and off for years and seemed mostly doting, not pressuring.

Had Manou and Ernst given up trying to communicate with and support each other emotionally?

Almost. But he seemed sweeter in the last few weeks.

The answers to these crucial questions were not to be found in police reports, radio news broadcasts, or doctors' observations. She crushed her fists to her head in self-recrimination. After almost two decades of marriage, she should have known him well enough to sense his state of mind and prevent this tragedy. And yet how could she have been aware of his mood that day? Every time problems arose between them or she asked about his actions or feelings, Ernst almost crouched in self-defense and fell into unyielding silence. His defiant impenetrability held power over her even in death.

As she heard the children awaken upstairs, Manou pressed her fingertips against her temples, pushing the unanswered questions into a corner of her mind, like memorabilia into a hatbox, for later reflection. For now, their family had to find ways to go on living without him.

Francis came into the kitchen first. At twelve, he still had his round child's face. He opened the refrigerator, took out eggs and bread, and put them on the counter. "I'll set the table if you'll make scrambled eggs and toast, Mom?"

"A good plan," Manou said softly, and she opened the refrigerator. The smell of toasting bread and butter melting in the frying pan warmed the room as Francis and Manou worked quietly together.

Karl came in next. He already had his coat on. "It will be a little while before I'm ready to go," Manou said.

"I don't need a ride. I'm going to walk to Jeff's house. He asked me if I could stay for dinner tonight. Can I?"

Manou thought for a minute. Did they all belong together or should the kids get on with life with their friends. The latter sounded the healthiest. "Sure," she agreed. "Call when you get there this afternoon, please."

"Okay," he said as he grabbed the first piece of toast from the toaster and slathered some jam on it.

"If he can go to Jeff's, can I have Beth over here after school?" Sophia said as she entered the kitchen. She had a sad face, swollen from tears, and it belied the typical breakfast chatter. Manou gave her a glass of orange juice and stroked her daughter's shoulder.

"Of course. Ready for some eggs and toast?"

She shrugged, "Yeah, I guess." Sophia sat at the table and began to read about her father's death in the paper.

"I'm going," called Karl as he walked heavily down the hall and out the front door.

While Manou poured the beaten eggs into the pan and scrambled them, Florence slid onto the chair next to her sister. "I'm too tired to go to school," she muttered.

Manou spooned portions of eggs onto four plates and added a slice of toast to each. "Francis, could you get these?"

Francis put breakfast plates in front of his sisters. "Here. Eat up." He got a third plate for himself, sat down, and stared at it. "I feel really tired, too," he admitted.

Manou stood behind Florence and pulled the child's tangled hair back away from her face. "It's the medicine Dr. Tremont gave you. You'll probably feel a little groggy for awhile."

"Gee," exclaimed Sophia angrily. "It says here that dad drowned under the truck. No way! He could swim better than anybody. I don't believe it, Mom."

"It doesn't really make sense but I'm afraid it's true."

"I'm not going to school," yelled Florence, and she burst into tears.

Manou pulled a chair next to her youngest child and leaned close to her. "Did I tell you Cindy called?"

"See, everyone will be making a big deal of this. I can't be saying yeah my dad died every two seconds all day."

"But sweetie, it's because they care."

"No they don't, they'll just think it's weird."

"I don't think so. Would you think it weird if Cindy's father died?"

Florence sniffed. "I'd think it was sad."

"That's exactly how she feels. Let her be a good friend to you. She'll make you feel better."

Florence nodded, sniffled, and they all ate without mentioning Ernst again. Manou would not pressure any of them to break their protective silence any more than she had forced Ernst to speak when he did not want to. This was the way of their family. Sensing the quiet misery of her children, Manou briefly felt angry with her husband for leaving her with more responsibility than she thought she could bear, but she quickly sent the emotion to the same subterranean place as her questions about the source of his breakdown, and she let herself fall into a safe fog of motherhood.

Over the next few weeks, Manou went through life mechanically, relying on Lucy and other friends to help with meals and organize the entire memorial service—except for the music. Manou knew exactly which piece the violinist from the college music department should play: Bach's Partita II in D minor. At first she wanted the whole piece played, but the funeral director advised her that it was too long and, since the audience would get restless, she should decide on one of the five movements. Considering the possibilities, Manou knew she wanted the music to express the complexity of Ernst's character and life, not just his last dark days. The first movement, Allemanda, was somber, slow, and appropriate for the circumstance, but simpler than the other movements. The second movement, Corrente, evoked the levity and joy of much of their relationship but was too cheerful for a memorial. The third and fourth movements, Sarabanda and Giga, each built melody, character, and mood but lacked a sense of completion. She concluded that although the first four movements reflected many facets of her husband, only the fifth, Ciaccona, the climactic conclusion to the partita, reflected the complexity of his life. It was long but the audience of Ernst's friends and colleagues would understand it. More importantly, it was Ernst's most beloved musical score, a masterpiece he had practiced endlessly one year until the whole family knew it by heart.

During the memorial, the soloist filled the Valley College chapel with notes that dove to oceanic depths then spiraled to the stars. Manou closed her eyes and allowed the violin to summon up the man she loved. She relived a moment Ernst played the Ciaccona just for her, under a desert night sky, when his musician's body and soul blended with every note. Manou ached in the depths of her being for the beautiful Ernst Feidler, a man who, like this solo piece for violin, was so passionate, baroque, and absolutely mysterious.

Corrente

The Running Dance

A week after the funeral, Inspector Kravitz brought Manou Ernst's personal effects, including his wallet. There was nothing in it but a twenty-deutschmark note, which only added to the mystery surrounding the circumstances of his death. How bizarre, she thought. Ernst always had at least a few dollars, pictures, credit cards, and a driver's license in his wallet, yet on the day of his death, he took nothing but one stained and stiff twenty-deutschmark note—and he hadn't been in Germany for months.

She asked a few questions about the investigation and learned that the police had found no drugs or alcohol in his system, no injury to his body, and no suicide note. The truck had been only half full of water and they discovered him underneath it as they dragged it from the canal. Kravitz also showed her a letter from a Professor Sorenson at Stanford. He had written that Ernst had been participating in laboratory research on hypnosis and applying it brilliantly to language proficiency but that his interest in hypnosis had been scientific, not personal, and Ernst had given no indication of emotional instability. Sorenson had noted, however, that Ernst had shown much sympathy for another graduate student who had recently drowned in a boating accident, although the event was not connected to Ernst's drowning. The police inquiry into his state of mind had effectively led nowhere, except perhaps to indicate Ernst's lack of attention while driving through the rainstorm, and thus his death had been officially classified as an "accidental drowning."

Manou saw no point in telling the inspector that her husband had been using hypnosis at home as part of his research or that he had been deeply upset by the student's drowning accident, even weeping about it one night after three Scotch-and-water cocktails that made him slur his speech. She was fed up with Inspector Kravitz's book of notes, in which he recorded details about Ernst's death like it was some kind of scientific research project. In her own mind, she continued trying to connect the pieces of the puzzle regarding Ernst's state of mind and final actions. She needed to understand how and why it had happened, in order to get beyond the pain and find hope for the future. After the inspector left, Manou brought Ernst's possessions upstairs. She tucked the wallet and his clothes into the deepest corner of a closet shelf.

As she stepped back, her foot brushed Ernst's violin case, propped against the closet wall. An electric current ran through her body, as if he himself had reached out and touched her. She jumped back and sat down heavily at the foot of the bed, staring at the violin case and reflecting on the past. When she had been young and the idea of death was so remote, and with life exuding from her every pore, she had been bewitched by Ernst's Wagnerian charm and seductive, mesmerizing violin playing. Now Manou was alone in the room that seemed as vacuous as her own being, and she feared that after all these years of living as a couple, there was no her without him.

Manou lived in a fog of incomprehension for days, but her responsibility to her children slowly brought her back to her present reality. She was determined to protect them, at all costs, from feeling that Ernst had abandoned them. She knew she was the only one to keep the ship of this family afloat. During the day, Manou maintained Ernst's lofty image and the routines of their lives, showing the resilience she and Ernst developed when they lived through World War II and later immigrated to America. They had both tended to throw themselves into action, to sculpt the present and future from the past.

But at night in the shadowy contours of their bedroom, Manou's resolve crumbled, and fear cut into her determination. She twisted and turned in bed, unable to calm her trembling heart until just before dawn, when she fell into an agitated sleep. She often dreamed of searching for his warm body in their cold bed, and then would awake abruptly with the realization that Ernst had been a deeply unhappy man.

Before he died, Manou had become frustrated with his unresponsiveness and lack of interest in doing things together. The assumptions and shared purpose that had validated their life together in the beginning became submerged under constant, frenetic activity. Ernst's relentless pursuits had erased time to spend together and share the big picture of their life with children, teaching, and personal dreams. Manou had given up trying to slow him down and mirrored his pace, precariously balancing her career and homemaking. They passed off the children like relay racers passing the baton. She could no longer distance herself from this failed pattern that seemed frantic and ruinous in hindsight.

Questions tormented Manou. Who was Ernst? When had she lost touch with him? And if he was a stranger, then who was that woman living with him year after year? Who was she now that he was gone? Who was Manou?

♪

A few weeks before she had met Ernst Feidler, while studying on a scholarship in Iowa in 1953, Marie Madeleine had dreamed about the wartime air raids that had pulled her out of her warm bed as a child ten years earlier in Nantes, permanently instilling in her a sense of stoicism. That winter, American bombs fell on Nantes and the Nazi antiaircraft guns retaliated. Her family had spent many nights in a cold bomb shelter, yet she never felt fear, never believed that they would die, or even be hit. The children had brought blankets, pillows, and homework, while the adults had brought wine and cards. Despite the fear of bombs, everyone had been funnier and nicer in the bomb shelter. The bonds came from their shared fate and an artificial sense of community created in the close quarters of the shelter. While in Iowa, Manou had wished that suffering through the relentlessly icy winter, cooped up in classrooms, would make her like Americans better, too, but it hadn't.

To help cope with the dreary situation, Manou had fallen back on a tried-and-true family remedy her mother always used in challenging circumstances: the "Méthode Coué," Doctor Émile Coué's positive-thinking strategy involving "optimistic autosuggestion." It employed the hypnotic chant "Every day, in every way, I am getting better and better." Her mother had used it both as a preventive and curative technique. For example, when Manou was sick, her mother would say, "When we are sick we must repeat, 'I am not sick. I am not sick.'" In the bomb shelter, she stated firmly, "No need to worry. We will be safe, safe, safe." As a child, Manou had bitterly resented this approach, wishing her mother would be gentler and more reassuring, saying things like, "Oh, chérie, I am so sorry you feel bad," or "I know you are scared. It will be over soon." But lacking any better approach in Iowa, Manou decided to try her mother's method, repeating, "Every day, in every way, I want to be in America. I want to be in America. I am not unhappy."

Perhaps the incantation had worked a little, because the truth was that Manou did want to be in America, even though she didn't like it much. At age twenty-two, she had come to America willingly because she found life in France unbearably rigid and routine.

As an athlete and a physical education major, Manou had qualified for a Fulbright scholarship to study in the United States, a country she knew little about other than the fact that it had saved France from Germany, with the mixed blessings of bombing raids and invasions. She envisioned the typical Hollywood movie imagery—skyscrapers, red rocks and wide deserts, gigantic sequoias, beaches lined with palm trees, people lounging elegantly by swimming pools, gangsters wielding machine guns, and enormous automobiles traveling on wide paved roads. Her parents simply said, "*Marie Madeleine, tu verras, les Américains sont de grands enfants.*" You'll see, Americans are big children.

On her application for the scholarship, Manou had neglected to specify *where* in America she wished to study. When she received her acceptance, she ran to her father's library to find Iowa on the map and was disappointed to discover that it was in the center of the United States, in the unglamorous Corn Belt. Nonetheless, she was determined to shed her old French skin and reinvent herself in a new country. She immediately applied for a student visa but learned a few days later that it had been denied. "*Mais pourquoi?*" she complained to a man with an ugly polka-dot tie and a bad haircut at the American Consulate.

He thumbed through her application folder with such slow deliberation that Manou almost jumped on his desk and grabbed it from him. Finally, he nodded. "Ah, I see you want to go to Iowa. Good choice. I grew up very near there." Looking inquisitively over his glasses, he added, "Nevertheless, there is a very serious problem. You are a Communist."

"*Mais non! C'est fou!* Are you crazy?"

"Did you or did you not travel behind the Iron Curtain in 1949?"

The Iron Curtain? Of course! She had gone with the French track team to participate in the World University Games in Budapest. "I traveled to Budapest as an athlete, but I am a physical education major, not a Communist," she answered him.

"That is not at all clear. There was a large Youth Communist Party rally the same week you were there. Perhaps your athletic adventure was a pretense."

What could she do? The Americans were completely unreasonable about Communism, with their Joseph McCarthy questioning everyone—movie stars, writers, and even ordinary shopkeepers.

"Listen," she told the consulate's assistant, "I am totally anti-Communist; so was my whole team. I can prove it. Let me tell you a funny story."

He looked skeptical and impatient so she spoke quickly. "We caught the train to Budapest and crossed into Hungary at a little border station. There were red flags everywhere, with the hammer and sickle emblem. The train stopped, and some officials climbed on board to check our papers. Everyone in Europe loves sports, east or west, so a crowd was at the station to greet us. But a military band was playing and it was raining, so everyone was very glum. The officials ordered us to sing a French song in honor of Communism. Everyone on the platform, even the children, waited for us to sing 'La Marseillaise,' but our delegation was, shall we say, mischievous."

Manou paused and drew a deep breath, and then continued, knowing her whole future was at stake. "We knew they wouldn't understand French so we sang the lyrics of a bawdy students' song to the tune of 'La Marseillaise':

My grandfather's balls are hanging over the staircase
And my grandmother is in despair to see them dry up,
For it was the most beautiful pair in the neighborhood.
You can come and admire them on the Fourteenth of July!

A French secretary snickered behind them, but the consulate's assistant was unresponsive. Manou persisted, "On our triumphant crescendo about the Fourteenth of July, the Hungarian military saluted grandfather's balls. We laughed all the way to Budapest." She paused. The consulate had no sense of humor. "We were making *fun* of the Communists. How could I *be* a Communist if I make fun of them?" Manou grinned hopefully at the man.

The Midwesterner didn't crack a smile but only slapped her folder on the desk and stated flatly, "Your visa has been denied."

Devastated, Manou knew she would have to find another way to get a visa—and very soon, because she was supposed to leave in the summer to practice English before starting classes at the University of Iowa.

While standing with her bike outside the consulate trying to decide what to do, she watched men in pressed suits exiting the oversized doors, shaking hands and slapping backs, and Manou realized she'd have to use connections to get her visa. The French Department of Immigration was just across the street, and when a young man exited, on impulse Manou called out, "Hey, *monsieur*, do you know people in there?" He gave a cocky grin that revealed he was pleased to be approached by an attractive young woman. She rode over to him and, with her hand outstretched, said, "*Bonjour*, I am Manou and I am having silly problems with a visa. I see you are from Immigration. Do you think you might help me?"

He straightened his shoulders like a man in charge and answered, "Perhaps. I'm in the processing department. Let's talk about it over coffee in, say, an hour. At the corner bistro?"

"*Bien sûr.* Your name is...?"

"Jacques."

She gave him a wave and pedaled down the street. Simone de Beauvoir might not have approved of her using her feminine wiles this way, but a little coffee with a handsome man in Immigration couldn't hurt her cause, and it might even be *très amusant*. She was, after all, an educated, popular athlete who would represent France abroad. Jacques would be pleased with the little flirtation and just might know someone higher up. And in fact, when she later had coffee with Jacques, he was amusing and did promise to write a letter to the American consulate on her behalf.

Her tactics paid off. After three months, letters of support from a government official who knew her father, an immigration official, and the head of the education department at the university helped Manou receive her visa, and she booked passage to New York on the *Mauretania II*, departing October 23, 1952. She would miss the beginning of the first semester, but she was still following her dream. On the day she embarked, her best friend, Claire, and Jacques from Immigration kissed her good-bye on both cheeks, gave her a bottle of champagne, and then they walked off arm in arm together. Manou felt a twinge of jealousy but also carefree anticipation of her own new adventures that lay ahead. Her parents were gloomy, but her mother had said with her best Méthode Coué voice, "You will have a good, good journey." Her parents were still waving good-bye when the ship spun to the starboard and steamed out of the port.

Manou thought she understood English—until her first day on the ocean liner. For six years, she had read Shakespeare and poetry and had written grammatically perfect essays in English in high school and university classes, but the students had never spoken a word of the language. While crossing the ocean, she first attributed her lack of comprehension to her excitement about being on the ship, with its two impressive red smokestacks and the white, black, and red trim around its massive hull, as well as hundreds of passengers strolling the decks. She had never traveled on a ship before and wandered the decks with the wide-eyed curiosity of a child. As she came out of the elegant dining room the first evening, carrying an apple, a steward flirted with her, pointing at the apple and saying, "Eve...Eve." She never understood his little joke and could barely comprehend any of the passengers' overtures either. Subsequently, Manou spent much time alone in her stateroom, seasick for most of the voyage because of the agitated October current.

Upon arrival in New York on November 3, 1952, she and thousands of others watched a giant board in Times Square tally up the victory of Dwight D. Eisenhower as president of the United States. Manou found New York City far more imposing than Paris, but she was no more afraid of it than she had been of bombs bursting above her in Nantes. Small things were perplexing, though, because she could understand only a fraction of what people were saying. In her hotel, she had no idea how to work the elevator and had to wait fifteen minutes until another guest pushed the "up" button, revealing the secret code. Her knowledge of Shakespearean English also was not helpful in the automat restaurant, where, jostled on all sides by New Yorkers in a rush, she put her money in the food machine and could not figure out how to get the items released from their little cages. Yet Manou sensed the optimism of the crowd on the streets because, as she could at least read in the newspapers, the general would set the course for a peace in Korea and prosperity for the post-war era.

A week later, poetry was definitley no help in communicating with Mr. Manner, the university foreign students' advisor who met Manou at the depot in Iowa City. She did her best to converse with him in single words, facial expressions, and crude invented hand signs. Worse, in her new classes she stammered pitifully, out of utter frustration, struggling to figure out what a teacher had said in one sentence when he was already on to the next. In France, Manou had been a good student accustomed to success and praise. She spoke Spanish in addition to her native language, so why was English so difficult? she wondered. In America, she felt frustrated, dumb, and discouraged, but was too proud to write her parents that she was ready to capitulate and come home.

Her Philippine roommate, Carmen, tried to help her by explaining weird sounds like *th* that contorted her French tongue. When she couldn't communicate, her defense strategy, as a good French woman, was to shake back her black hair, wave a dismissive hand in the air, look down her aquiline nose, and retreat haughtily into a shell. To survive her culture shock, Manou focused on observing the peculiar American way of life and criticizing it to Carmen, saying at one point, "They ask stupid questions about France. Their parties are so dreary, everyone just standing around shaking ice in glasses. And football! How boring to watch men with fat thighs butt each other like ugly goats!"

She also wrote Claire long letters:

Dear Claire,

This one you won't believe! Last weekend I was invited with a group of foreign students to visit a dairy farm in a nearby village. The tour guide was showing us sparkly clean machinery, explaining processes, pointing to cartons advancing on rollers like a well-disciplined army, when she suddenly turned to me and asked, "Do you know about pasteurization in France?" I was shocked! These Americans think they have invented everything and we are still in the Middle Ages. Can you believe people here ask me whether we have radios in France and have ever heard

of television? Unfortunately, my English is still too limited to give smart, ironic
replies. So I just nod and wait until I can write you the details, hoping to make
you laugh . . .

My best to Jacques. I hope you are finding him very amusing.

Love, Marie Madeleine

As Manou learned more English, people were charmed by her accent, poise, and beauty and invited her to parties. There, she was often quizzed about the American liberation of her country, the women asking, "What did you do when the GIs entered your city? Did you fall into their arms?"

"I was only fourteen," Manou would reply demurely.

After a few martinis, the men would break out in a chorus of a naughty trench song:

Oh, Mademoiselle from Armentières,
parlez-vous.
You didn't have to know her long,
To know the reason men go wrong!
 Hinky dinky, parlez-vous.

At the time, American college girls rarely participated in sports, so when Manou went to the track in her red shorts and pale blue T-shirt to jump hurdles just for exercise, young men sniggered at the sight. Manou had always been athletic, ever since she and her sister had spent summers at their grandparents' home in the country, joyfully running through the fields doing cartwheels and headstands. Eventually, the local paper heard about the lovely female French athlete and asked to photograph her jumping a hurdle in her sports attire and in contrasting poses—such as in an evening gown. After Carmen lent her an embroidered shawl to wear with a black skirt and white blouse for the photo session, they had a great laugh when the photos were published side-by-side on the front page over a caption that claimed she wore an "exclusive Parisian gown."

"Who would know the difference?" Manou had said to Carmen at the time. "In this country people don't know any more about dress than about how to cook. They have no idea what good food tastes like!"

Carmen, who had been studying in Iowa a couple of years and didn't mind American ways, had told her, "You can't complain about everything, Manou. It's really not so bad once you get used to it."

Dear Claire,

I am so glad you and Jacques are enjoying nightlife in Paris. The restaurant
you described makes me drool! The food here is atrocious. Last weekend I was
invited to dinner for Thanksgiving, one of the big American holidays, at a farm in

Osage, a small town in northern Iowa. Imagine a dry turkey served with a very sweet sauce made from red berries ("cranberries," they call them) along with sweet potatoes and corn. Yes, you read it right, corn! Like the stuff we feed chickens.

But I confess I have mixed feelings about these people. They were so nice and had gone to so much trouble. I felt sorry for them, even though they enjoyed the meal very much. I have been thinking of my cousin lately, the one who lives in Paris and who always says, "Why should I go look for something else in a foreign country? We have the best of everything here in France." Well, I tend to agree with him on that point. Sometimes I am tempted to give up.

It is hard being away. I miss you; I miss my family. I don't want to tell them, though. They would be too happy to say, "We told you to stay home." But I must go on, don't you think?

Love, Marie Madeleine

The attention Manou began receiving in Iowa made her briefly feel good, and proud. But then came Christmas, a holiday she considered garish, with its overabundance of lights and tacky Santas and reindeer. Worse, in January she received horrible grades and would have purchased a plane ticket back to Paris if it hadn't been for the Méthode Coué. Periodically, Manou clenched her teeth while crossing campus in the bitter cold and recited, "Every day, in every way, I like America better and better."

But not even the Méthode Coué would have bolstered her enough had she not discovered the Center for Foreign Students, or CFS. It was a small, warm lounge with a tiny kitchenette where foreigners created an international atmosphere, cooked food from their homelands, and laughed together about American customs. There she met people from all over the world, who were studying physics, biology, literature, and even theater. Their conversations had the scope and conviviality of café life in Paris, as they talked long into the night. When Manou tiptoed into her dorm room late one evening, Carmen mumbled from her bed, "I guess you feel at home now." Manou pulled the covers over her head against the cold air of the poorly heated building and, for the first time in weeks, forgot to recite her evening prayer: "Every day, in every way..."

At the CFS she met several other students and teachers from France, including the head of the French department, Charles Baptiste. During a short-lived flirtation, she discovered he was married, but he offered her a job as a teaching assistant for his French I and French II classes. After Manou made it clear she wouldn't have an affair with a married man and wanted no strings attached to the job, he smiled and said, "Too bad. It would have been fun. But I still want you to teach." She was thrilled because it meant she would get credit, earn money, and, thank God, speak French every day.

A Norwegian music student and pianist named John Lund took one of her French classes, and Manou found him very attractive. She expected John to ask her on a date, and one day when there was a call for her in the dormitory, she was delighted as she ran to the phone thinking it was a call from him.

"Hello, is this Manou?" a deep voice asked in perfect French.

"Yes, speaking," she answered still assuming it was John.

"This is Ernst Feidler." He stated this as if she surely would know who he was.

"Who?"

"I've seen you around campus. I'm John Lund's friend. Would you like to go out with me for coffee?"

"American coffee? No thanks!" Manou laughed.

"How about a walk in the snow?"

She didn't want to hurt his feelings, but she would have preferred a call from John. "Too cold. I'm from the Mediterranean, you know."

"Yes, I know."

"Perhaps sometime we can talk at the CFS instead."

"I am certain we will," he said with undaunted assurance.

Ernst called her several more times that week, but she declined each of his invitations. She asked around and found out that he was a German studying languages, which explained his talent for speaking flawless French, and he also played violin in duets with John in the music department. When he eventually came to the French department with John and introduced himself, Manou realized that she had previously noticed his good looks at the CFS. He had soft blond hair, an athletic body, and, as she knew from the phone calls, a vibrant voice. Close up, she was drawn to his magnetic blue eyes that opened wide with complete attention one minute then looked away, removed, the next. There was a physical confidence and intensity about him that fascinated Manou, and his appeal was only heightened by a delicate little scar on his left cheek that he got, she learned later, in a fencing match as a university student. Ernst's scar suggested vulnerability behind his self-assurance that made her feel tenderness toward him. Manou had never felt tenderness for a man—attraction, mystery, lust, fear, disdain, and jealousy, yes—but never tenderness.

She finally agreed to go for a walk with Ernst. As they left the center, she caught him grinning at John.

"What was that about?" she wanted to know.

"Nothing, nothing," insisted Ernst, though he couldn't hide a smile. "Oh, all right. We had a little wager," he confessed.

She eyed him with suspicion and demanded, "What kind of wager?"

"I bet that I'd get you to go out with me."

Manou started to protest but stopped, realizing it had just been a good-humored boyish prank. "I guess you won the big prize, didn't you," she quipped.

He took her arm and answered, "I certainly did."

Manou and Ernst talked enthusiastically, both bored with Iowa City and starved for stimulating conversation. To them, American students seemed to focus mostly on football games and beer parties, unaware that there was an intriguing world outside their hometown. They discovered they shared a love for hiking, swimming, and music.

"Why did you come here?" Ernst asked her.

She laughed and answered, "I thought I was going to Hollywood," not wanting to give the simplistic answer that she normally gave—that she was looking for "experience abroad" and "opportunity in America." She paused then added, "I love my family, but they are weighed down by their war experience. I lived through it, too, but now I need a different kind of life, one more hopeful and lighter."

Ernst nodded sympathetically. "As a German, it is nearly impossible to gain distance from Hitler anywhere in Europe. It's difficult here, too, but at least this country is very big."

It intrigued Manou that, with distance from Europe, she and a German could be friends and that they could share perspective rather than clash. "America is a strange combination of open and closed, isn't it? I came to study physical education but people keep talking to me about Chanel perfume and chic Parisian fashion. Men generally act like a woman can't walk across the street, much less run a few miles."

As they crossed the university campus, she asked him, "And you? What do you want to do?"

"I love the violin, you know. I've studied music since I was a boy."

"Music is important to me, too." Manou told him. "One of my neighbors played his flute in the bomb shelter during raids. As long as he was playing, I wasn't afraid, and after the war, I joined a music club to learn the names of the compositions I liked and what had inspired the composers."

"I couldn't live without playing." Ernst paused thoughtfully. "But I wouldn't want to be one of twenty violinists in an orchestra, or even second violinist. I'm still not certain exactly how to achieve a career as a soloist."

"Why don't you become a music major?" Manou asked. "Then you could play all the time."

"That's true. But there are so many other things I'm interested in, like Russian, French, other languages, psychology." He looked at her with a grin. "And a sweet French woman."

In spite of their winter malaise, culture shock, and language barriers, Manou and Ernst felt the inexhaustible promise of their chosen country. And they soon fell in love.

As crested irises and Lenten roses replaced snow, the two left the flat campus for hikes on the bluffs along the Iowa River, swollen with snowmelt, fearlessly climbing dangerous precipices out of sheer exhilaration. While they hiked, they sang songs together, Ernst teaching German summer camp songs to Manou while she taught him French Alpine hiking tunes.

Whenever possible, Manou attended Ernst's duet performances with John. She especially loved their interpretation of Schubert's Fantasy for Violin and Piano in C major because it rose to a finale in which Ernst could move his whole body with fiery strokes of the bow. John's Nordic constraint balanced Ernst's Germanic vigor in Grieg's Sonata in C major, where John's firm keystrokes offset Ernest's passionate rendering of the melody toward the center of the movement. At every performance she attended, Manou wanted them to play forever.

One evening, after John and Ernst played a sonata for piano and violin by Franz Shubert, Ernst took her to his off-campus room and they made love under the spell of the music. He delighted in her uninhibited affection yet after love making, he was unusually quiet. His silence made her nervous so she chatted nervously about inconsequential events of the day while she dressed. Before she put on her coat, he turned toward her and asked, "I'm not the first, am I?"

Manou sat back on the bed and paused before she answered. French men liked experienced women. American men were crude in their advances but always claimed they wanted to marry a virgin. Manou wasn't certain what Ernst thought. She decided honesty was the only way to find out.

"My first lover was another French athlete who was on the team that went to the World Games in Budapest."

"First?"

"Yes, and you are the second. If this is a problem," she stood up, "then you should take me home now and not call me again."

Ernst scowled, and then he got up and dressed in silence. They walked from his house through a quiet neighborhood to the university. By the time they stood on the doorstep of her dormitory, he gave her a gruff hug, said, "I'll call you tomorrow," and walked quickly away into the dark.

Ernst called her the next afternoon, did not mention their conversation about virginity, and asked her out to a movie as if nothing had happened. Manou and Ernst began going to parties and became a popular, handsome European couple. Manou stopped writing to Claire about irritating American customs.

Ernst and I found a romantic little café in Iowa City that played music from Moulin Rouge in the background. We laughed because in spite of our highbrow taste in music, we sang along with the verse "The greatest thing you'll ever learn is just to love, and be loved in return."

Soon Manou was able to pronounce difficult words like *sheet* and *beach* correctly, instead of them sounding like "shit" and "bitch," which had made students snicker. And her grades improved. In January, the university had been an alien planet to Manou; by June, it felt like home. After final exams in late May, Carmen left for the Philippines, and Ernst and Manou enjoyed the privacy of her empty dorm room, where they made love lazily in the late afternoons, watching the sunset through the window. Afterwards, the two young athletes would go to the university swimming pool to swim laps and frolic in the water.

There was a walkway over the middle of the pool that separated the shallow water from the deep. Swimmers had to walk around it or dive under it. One evening, Manou did some dives off the board into the deep end while Ernst swam around the shallow end. When she was up on the board, he waved to her and then dove underneath the walkway. Manou did a swan dive off the board and expected to meet him in the middle. She surfaced but he wasn't there. She tread water for a minute or two and began to get anxious. Just as she was about to call for help, he shot out of the water in front of her, gasping for air with a tense, fierce smile.

"Ernst, you frightened me," she scolded.

He swam in a slow circle around her catching his breath. "Oh, that was nothing. I can stay under for at least five minutes. We trained for that in the *Hitlerjugend*, the Hitler youth corps."

Manou swam to the edge of the pool, lifted herself gracefully onto the edge, and sat with her feet dangling in the water. She had heard of the youth brigades that fought in some of the last horrible battles of World War II. They were known for being ferocious, fanatical fighters. "Did you have to fight?" she asked cautiously, not really wanting to dredge up the old war.

Ernst rested his elbows on the side of the pool next to her. "Every boy in my town had to participate in the youth corps. At first, it was fun. When I was thirteen, we went to special military training camps for three weeks. They had us sing together, 'We are the soldiers of the future.'" He paused and shrugged. "They taught us how to handle pistols, machine-guns, and hand-grenades. They taught us to stay under water as long as possible to put dynamite charges under bridges."

"Did you go to Normandy like the others?"

"No, I was too young to go." Ernst pulled himself up next to Manou. "The sixteen- and seventeen-year-olds became the 12th SS-Panzer Division Hitlerjugend and went to France to fight the Americans. We had a chant that went 'Many die. Many are born.' I wanted to go to Normandy."

Manou took his hand. "I'm glad you didn't."

"Instead I stayed home and dug trenches," he said bitterly. Ernst wiped the water off his face and shook his hair. "When the war ended, those of us still left in town had to tell the American military tribunals all about the youth corps. At first, I hated them, but they were kind, smart, respectful towards me, and did not scorn us Hitlerjugend as if we were bad dogs, like the Russians did. It was hard to stay angry."

"You were smart."

"They showed me how we had been duped into serving the Fuehrer. They said it was a crime against humanity." He turned and stared hard at her. "Now here I am in America. It's strange, isn't it?"

She smiled at him and watched his face soften. "We're here," she said. "We are beginning again here."

At the end of the last week of school, Manou told him, "Professor Baptiste said the school won't pay for a summer assistant. My parents will want me to come home. After I correct my students' exams, I'll probably have to go." She paused, and then asked, "Will you go back to Germany?"

"Of course not." He stroked her arm. "Manou, don't leave."

"Then what shall I do?"

Ernst propped himself up on his elbow and asked, "Do you want to go back to France?"

"Absolutely not! Not right now, anyway."

"And I don't want to go back to Germany." They stared at each other until he grinned and suggested, "Then let's be *real* Americans."

"What on earth do you mean?"

"What is the biggest image of Americans?"

"Cowboys, of course."

"And where do cowboys live?"

"They live in the West."

"And how did they get there?"

"In wagons. *Mon Dieu*! You don't mean we'll...?"

He laughed so hard it brought tears to his eyes. "West. Let's go West! I've wanted to go to California forever, and there must be plenty of jobs and schools out there."

"Ah, oranges and the ocean. That does sound wonderful, but honestly, how would we get there?"

He kissed her and said, "In an *uncovered* wagon—an American convertible."

Inspired by his sense of whimsy and adventure, Manou wrote her parents a vague letter about her plans to go to California with a German "friend." As she suspected, her father answered with a diatribe against Hitler. Ernst wrote something similar to his parents and received an eloquent dissertation about the evils of Napoleon. Being French and German, the lovers were supposed to be mortal enemies, yet for them, unlike their parents, the war was over. Europe represented the past, and they were looking toward the future and felt invincible. It didn't bother them that they had no job prospects and no idea what life would be like in Los Angeles. They had a destination and trusted that the journey to the Pacific Ocean would be a grand adventure.

Manou had some savings from her teaching job, and for one hundred dollars, they bought a sleek, elegant 1939 black LaSalle convertible with worn red leather seats. Ernst donned a white fedora that made him look like a blond Clark Gable as he drove the car away from the dealer's lot. In the middle of June, they loaded it with all their earthly possessions: clothes, a record player and records, Ernst's violin, a typewriter, a couple of books, a blanket, and picnic food. Then with ninety-seven dollars, they climbed in and left Iowa City in anticipation of a great quest and with unshakeable faith in their love.

At the end of their first hot, dusty day on the road, they slept on a blanket on hard ground under the stars. On the second day, they had a flat tire. Dripping with sweat, Ernst wrestled the old bolts off the wheel. Rude truck drivers slowed and gaped as they passed but never offered to help. Manou, using a broken umbrella for shade, tried to lighten the ordeal by making wry observations about them, like "There's a man who has enough grease in his hair to loosen your bolts."

As they drove past endless cornfields in Iowa and Nebraska, the thrill of the adventure slowly devolved into reality. Day after day, they ate rubbery white-bread-and-jam sandwiches with lukewarm milk, trying to make their minuscule bankroll last until LA. Some mornings they had to push the elegant old car to get it started. Evenings the smell of burning hot asphalt rose up like steam through the car's floorboards. Once, in an attempt to help Ernst cope with the challenges, Manou told him about her mother's technique for surviving adversity, and she began reciting the litany "Every day, in every way, things will get better." Ernst gave her such a disgusted look that she tried to cover up her hurt by whistling a melody from a Mozart violin concerto she'd heard Ernst and John perform. To her relief, Ernst launched into a commentary about different violins in Mozart's time, telling her how orchestral violins had been constructed to sound "silvery" and concert violins to have a "human voice," depending on the thickness of the top of the instrument.

"I once played a two-hundred-year-old baroque concert violin at the university in Munich. It was so different from the classical violins today," Ernst mused.

"In what way?" Manou asked. She wasn't especially interested, but at least the topic of music had softened his mood.

"Modern classical instruments are all built in an identical form, leaving little to chance," Ernst said, assuming a professorial tone. "The rhythms of Bach's partitas, for example, were those of very well-known folk dances from Germany, Italy, and Spain. With the concert violin, he could tease his own meaning out of the simple chord progressions and create something completely new." He gazed pensively toward the empty horizon ahead of them and continued, "The baroque violin was really built for the soloist. I wish I had such a jewel. I could speak through its strings."

"And what would you say?"

"I'd speak of all the great themes of human experience that have no real words, like fear, betrayal, love, joy, even death. I can only say these things through music. It is my voice." Ernst frowned abruptly and looked away from her, as if he had said too much. Gazing out the side window, he announced, "Look, there's a lake. Let's stop and swim."

The lake was really a small green pond, but they were grateful because it was cool and refreshing. They washed the grit and perspiration off their athletic bodies, splashed through the lily pads along the shore, and chased water turtles to the opposite bank. Manou got out first and, sitting on the grass to dry her hair, watched Ernst swim like Tarzan through the jade-colored water, admiring the rippling strength of his shoulders as he circled the pond.

Continuing west, Manou and Ernst discussed differences between the American and European landscapes as they sped past endless tall-grass prairies undulating like choppy seas and foaming with floral plumes. The immense open spaces all the way to the horizon overwhelmed them, prompting a mixture of ecstasy and fear. The lack of physical boundaries made them feel like they were at last free of limitations. Then they climbed high into the Colorado Rockies, with the old car smoking, forcing them to stop every few miles to add water. Just when Manou began to worry that the LaSalle would never get them to the promised land, the landscape distracted her with its stunning peaks, gaping canyons, cascading rivers, magnificent aspen trees covering the mountainsides in a pale green hue, and lush wild irises along creek banks. So awestruck were they that they took a wrong turn in northern Colorado and, instead of driving directly to Utah, ended up on a deserted road in southern Wyoming.

With darkness descending and nothing but rocky desert surrounding them, they pulled over, and Ernst rolled out their blanket while Manou laid out their last scraps of bread, jam, and warm milk. Soon the sunset engulfed the distant hills in red and gray, and, for lack of anything better to do, they decided to celebrate its beauty. Shattering the quiet isolation of the vast empty Wyoming desert, Ernst and Manou began to sing songs from their childhoods, their voices spinning off into the silence while night fell, slowly illuminated by a full moon and a million stars.

Finally, Ernst pulled out his violin and began to play. He leaned lovingly into his instrument and swayed in the moonlight, his body, losing its hard edges, transfigured into a tapestry of motion and sound. Manou witnessed a part of his soul she had never before encountered, the hidden voice he could not express with words. His music alternately sobbed for the powerlessness of the human condition and aspired boldly to all potentialities. Stopping, he whispered, "That was the Ciaccona, the last movement of Bach's Partita II. Someday I'll play the whole piece perfectly." He lightly stroked the body of his violin and proclaimed, "I'll be another Jascha Heifetz, you'll see."

At that moment, Manou had no doubt she was listening to a virtuoso. "I know you will," she decreed with absolute faith.

Long into the night, they talked about their future. He wanted to live by the sea, he said, to have children and become a great violinist. Manou wanted him to know her intimately so she revealed her secrets about the first man she had slept with, what her life had been like during the war, and how strange it was to be in love with a German after having witnessed French women having their heads shaved for collaborating with the enemy. She also confessed that she was sometimes afraid of losing Ernst, or of losing herself in her love for him. Opening up like this was a sweet surrender.

Instead of speaking in turn about his childhood or his first loves, Ernst kissed her and enchanted her with a Brahms lullaby. Her own aspirations, insubstantial compared to his grave devotion to music, were swept away into the vast Wyoming night as love for Ernst flooded every pore of her body.

The next day, the barren desert gave way to the red rock country of Utah. They pushed on to the Great Salt Lake, which seemed uninviting after the cool waters of the Rockies, and the city on its shores too imposing. Driving south into Arizona, they slept in the car near a railroad track and were awakened periodically by coyote cries and passing trains. At one point, Ernst jerked out of the blankets, sweating, and woke Manou with a hoarse plea: "Get him away from me."

"Who, *mon amour?*"

"The beast. He's come to get me." He pointed a trembling hand into the dark. "See? The yellow eyes. The red tongue."

Manou squinted into the dark and replied, "I don't see anything. Is it a coyote?"

"No, no. A man, a goat, maybe, with cloven hooves. I don't know," Ernst whispered.

The image of the yellow-eyed beast was so vivid that it disturbed Manou. He did not normally express such flights of the imagination, playing or dreaming, so she stroked his forehead and pulled him back down next to her, reassuring them both by saying, "It was just a dream, nothing more." Ernst shook under the blankets even as Manou wrapped her arms around his chest until he fell back asleep.

The next day, Ernst woke in a sullen mood. The sand and heat seemed endless through Nevada. The radiator kept boiling over, so they loaded gallons of water in the backseat and stopped every ten miles to replenish the coolant. At one rusty gas stop, a rattlesnake coiled up by the pump. Ernst filled the tank and jumped in ready to roll, but the LaSalle wouldn't start. He lost his temper at the old clunker, kicked the tires, and yelled, "Dieses ist American junk. I hate this trip, and I won't drive another mile."

Manou was stunned. His response to stress was usually cool silence, which frustrated her, but it was preferable to such a tantrum. "Ernst, calm down," she muttered, more than a little irritated.

His eyes glared and he shouted, "No woman tells me what to do. Maybe you should just catch a bus back to Iowa. I'm sure you'd charm some other man in an instant, Marie Madeleine." Then he stormed back to the gas station.

Manou was stunned that he would insult her like that and hurt that he considered her fickle and manipulative. "I will not cry, I will not cry," she ordered herself as she crossed the street to a diner.

"You okay, honey?" the waitress asked as she set down a menu and a glass of water. "Fight with your sweetie? Happens to me all the time." She gestured back toward a man in the kitchen in a soiled white apron.

"I'm perfectly fine. I'd like a Coke and a cheese sandwich."

Manou spent the afternoon watching Ernst through the diner's plate-glass window. Ernst and the gas station mechanic pushed the car into the garage, and Ernst stubbornly leaned on a wall outside the garage in the heat, waiting for the starter to be fixed. By dusk, the car had been repaired, and Ernst pulled up calmly to the diner and waved at her to get in the passenger seat. Manou, climbing in, reflected on the fact that she had now seen two aspects of her lover that upset her: her controlled Wagnerian god dreamt of frightening creatures and he had a propensity to launch missiles of cruel judgment.

Manou approached Los Angeles on an emotional edge. On the one hand, she knew the sea was just over the hills and they had reached their destination, manifesting their dream to get to the West Coast. On the other hand, they only had forty-five dollars left, and they were dirty, exhausted, and bitter from their argument. Adding to their gloom, they lost their way in the web of freeways around the city and had to spend another night in the cramped car.

The next day, they left the freeway and drove along miles of look-alike streets lined with small dusty houses and yards burnt by the sun. Ernst finally pulled over to the curb and shut off the engine.

"We don't know a single soul here," Manou whined. "How are we going to survive in a big, unknown city without family or friends?"

Ernst replied coldly, "Maybe we should have thought of that earlier."

Afraid of another outburst from him, Manou crossed her arms tightly against her chest and turned to watch a group of children kicking a ball along the sidewalk.

After ten minutes of paralyzing silence, Ernst lurched out of the LaSalle, slammed the door behind him, and marched up to a newsstand. Then he climbed back in the driver's seat with a newspaper and snapped it open against the steering wheel, concluding, "There is only one thing to do. Find work." After a few minutes of reading the classifieds, he added, "Manou, we'll survive. We always do." He folded the paper, pulled the LaSalle back into the street, and drove several more blocks until reaching an old brick building with a chipped sign that read, "The Roosevelt Hotel."

They carried their little suitcases across a stained linoleum floor, paid the balding, unshaven clerk, and climbed three flights to a shabby room with a squeaky iron bed and a nicked bureau. The bathroom was down the hall. Manou collapsed onto the mattress and sighed. "At least it's not the backseat of the car."

The next morning, over breakfast at a greasy diner down the street from the hotel, they scoured the classifieds and agreed that the only work available for Ernst was as a door-to-door salesman, paid on commission. He signed in at the one-room office of the Orthopedic Mattress and Box Spring Factory near the railroad tracks, got his assignment and a demo mattress, and drove to the designated neighborhood. Manou followed along in the LaSalle, waiting in the car while he carried the mattress from one porch to the next.

At each stop, Ernst recited a long speech to the lady of the house: "How do you do, ma'am? How are you on this fine day? My name is Ernst Feidler. I am the advertising manager with the Orthopedic Mattress Factory. I am not a salesman, and I am not here to sell you anything, so you can relax. My purpose in calling on you is merely to demonstrate the Orthopedic Mattress and Box Spring and to explain the details about what goes into making up this set. If I find that you fit in with our advertising plan, I can work out a nice factory deal for you whereby I'll put an Orthopedic Mattress and Box Spring in your home at a special factory price with no money down. We'll give you a piggy bank in which to put away forty cents a day, and that will pay for your set. Do you see what I mean, ma'am?

"It is important to have the box spring as well as the mattress, otherwise it will be like putting a brand new Cadillac on top of old tires, or wearing a new dress with old shoes. Do you understand, ma'am?"

Knowing that Ernst must be finding the job ridiculous and humiliating, Manou kept his spirits up by winking at him from the car each time he moved on to the next house. Although the ladies usually welcomed him into their homes graciously and listened politely, he never sold a single mattress. Once he even had a cup of coffee with a housewife and admitted that the last thing she needed was an Orthopedic Mattress and Box Spring. After three days, Ernst knew beyond a doubt that he was no salesman and quit.

The lovers made light of Ernst's attempts at salesmanship, but their apprehension about not being able to make a living in California grew. Ernst tried to reassure Manou, saying, "Other people become rich and famous in this part of the country. Why not us?" But they knew they had to do something quickly. They only had five dollars left.

At a gas station, Ernst met a Dutchman who, after listening to their tale of woe, gave Ernst ten dollars for his watch, which they used to buy bread, a quart of milk, and one last night at the Roosevelt. Passing the milk bottle back and forth as they relaxed on the bed, they realized they'd have to sell the record player and the records next. Like convicts eating their last meal, they plugged in the Victrola and indulged in an orgy of classical music: Beethoven, Mozart, Brahms, Saint-Saëns. Transported by a particularly beautiful cadenza of the Paganini Concerto No. 1, they made love in an orchestral crescendo, pushing reality away a little longer.

The next morning, completely broke, they moved everything into the LaSalle. When they drove away from the Roosevelt, the engine rattled, sounding like a marble had fallen into the air filter, and Ernst and Manou looked at each other as if it were doomsday. At a pawnshop, they only got ten dollars for their record player and records. Heartbroken, they parked and walked up Grand Avenue asking about work in every store and gas station. One shopkeeper told Ernst a circus manager was looking for extras to wear a lion's head or a horse's head in an upcoming parade. Ernst wrote down the address, just in case. They spent the night in the car at a gas station, where the attendant let them park and use the bathroom. Manou wept in exhaustion and exasperation but swore that she still trusted Ernst to work out a solution.

As they continued searching for work the next morning, they crisscrossed La Cienega Avenue in South Los Angeles, looking for addresses in the classifieds, only to find locked doors or jobs filled. As they were driving away from a hardware store, they passed a large dilapidated old house with a sign in the yard that advertised "Help Wanted: Maintenance." Manou and Ernst went up the shaky wooden steps to the front door and knocked. The door opened a sliver. "Yeah?" asked a man with watery eyes that disappeared in a face marred with acne scars and swollen from alcohol abuse.

"We're responding to your sign."

"Right. Right. I'm Jack Lawry. Come on in." He swung the door wide and yelled into the back of the house, "Edith, git out here." A woman hustled down the hall toward them. She resembled a sick, skinny little mouse, gray and all dried up. This odd couple sat Ernst and Manou down in a dark parlor and explained the job. They managed seven cottages for an absentee landlord, and they asked Ernst and Manou if they would be interested in cleaning and repairing the cottages in exchange for room and board in the big house. The young couple was thrilled at the apparently perfect solution to their dilemma.

The small, hot room Edith showed them had a tiny chest of drawers, a gas burner, and another narrow iron bed with a thin mattress—definitely not an Orthopedic Mattress and Box Spring. That night Edith served them overcooked chicken, watery mashed potatoes, and scalded green beans, food that Ernst and Manou, who had long since given up complaining about American cuisine, found hot and filling.

The next day, Jack instructed them to start painting the exterior of the cottages. Ernst poured white paint into a shallow tray and rolled a fresh coat over the siding, while Manou covered the window trim and door jambs with dark green paint. After the exteriors were done, they tackled the interiors with assorted cans of cheap paint of whatever color happened to be on sale that Jack had bought. They painted ten hours a day for weeks, yet, despite the drudgery, remained optimistic, glad to have food to eat and a roof over their heads. To keep themselves going, they sang, finding pleasure, as always, in music.

Late one afternoon, when they were both exhausted and dizzy from the turpentine fumes, Ernst stood on a ladder, covered in blue paint like a creature from a spooky lagoon, and, angrily wielding his paintbrush over his head, said, "This is probably how it all started for Hitler." With that, they collapsed on the floor in laughter, shaking their heads at their strange trajectory from college students to indentured servants.

"I love you for this," Manou said, kissing Ernst's smeared cheek.

"For slapping ugly paint on rundown cottages?" he asked.

"No, Ernst. For your irony and humor. For making it light for us no matter what."

After they had finished painting the cottages, they began cleaning them, scrubbing old toilets and greasy ovens, work that was humiliating and anything but romantic. And their bosses also became gradually less bearable. Jack and Edith, realizing they'd found a goldmine of youthful energy, devised grand projects to take advantage of Ernst and Manou's labor, as if their tenants were servants or sharecroppers. Edith, for her part, spent most of the time in the kitchen, out of Jack's way. And while the couple rarely argued openly, Manou noticed that once in a while Edith's lips were swollen and her cheeks bruised purple and green.

After seeing how hard they worked, Jack was full of big ideas about how they could make money together. He suggested they sell used tools from town to town. Ernst and Manou would do most of the work, but they would all reap rewards. Jack never asked if they were really married but gave them cheap rings, saying, "It ain't right for married people not to wear them," and Edith gave them used clothes.

While Ernst and Manou admitted to some misgivings about their strange familial relationship with Jack and Edith, they didn't talk about how discouraged they were feeling. Instead, they masked it by repeating how in love they were. Ernst had brooding silent spells that made Manou uneasy, but she was afraid to question him about them. Sometimes she felt his moodiness could undermine their hopes for a better life in LA, but she convinced herself that he was entitled to his feelings and that his brooding was only temporary.

At one point, they scanned the classifieds for other jobs and came across an agency seeking women to pose for photos in a bathing suit. Manou thought it sounded simple and promising, especially since the pay was good. Jack thought it sounded fishy and insisted that the men accompany her to the studio. They found Studio Five in an old warehouse in a shabby neighborhood. The man at the desk looked Manou up and down and told her to come back at 7:00 p.m.

That evening, Manou returned. Several women were already waiting outside, dressed in tight skirts, fishnet stockings, and jersey tops that pinched their waists and revealed canyons of cleavage. They all looked at her in a strange way and snickered, knowing she didn't belong there in her tidy blue skirt and worn blouse. Suddenly, Manou realized that the women could be walking down the notorious Rue St. Denis in Paris and abruptly left, opting not to join the oldest profession in the world.

The episode unleashed another dark mood on Ernst. That night he turned away from her and promptly fell asleep. Manou lay awake feeling gullible to have taken the ad seriously. She imagined her mother's face if she had seen Studio Five. Her mother had refused to talk to her children about sexuality, except to hiss in disgust at the way French women threw themselves at the American GIs after Patton had driven the occupiers across the Rhine. Manou had always been involved in physical activity, especially sports, and so following her sexual instincts made sense to her. She wasn't promiscuous, but by the time she left for America on the *Mauritania* she'd had a lover, a fact she never divulged to her rigid parents. And while she had told Ernst about her boyfriend, she immediately regretted it, not because Ernst was a prude in bed—on the contrary, he was an enthusiastic lover—but because of his frequent snide remarks about her "wanton" behavior.

They awoke the next morning and for days thereafter increasingly discouraged about their prospects. Jack and Edith continued to make constant demands on them, and during the restless hot summer nights, their neighborhood was often the scene of wild parties or knife fights. They would lie in bed sweating and listening to breaking bottles, loud music, and drunken voices. Worse, the LaSalle's rattle had become a death knoll, and one evening, when it broke down completely, spewing black smoke, Ernst abandoned it by the curb.

Lacking transportation, they felt imprisoned in Jack and Edith's gloomy house. Why did they feel trapped? Manou wondered. Was it fear? Inertia? A strange form of bondage? They had discovered neither Disneyland or Hollywood; there was nothing but nonstop work. Los Angeles seemed to be smothering them with its lack of opportunity and its octopus of freeway tentacles.

Aware of the couple's wavering enthusiasm, Jack and Edith gave them a day off and directions to Hermosa Beach by bus. After riding west for an hour, they discovered the beautiful and nearly empty shore, where they spent the rest of the day in the sun, intermittently swimming in huge waves and washing all responsibility off their overburdened young shoulders. Soon they felt whole again.

Despite the restful day off, Ernst and Manou continued to feel the American Dream was beyond their reach, and they conspired to get away from the job at Jack's house. Often they skipped out to check the classifieds before their keepers woke up, but the alternatives to working with Jack and Edith mainly involved selling merchandise door-to-door: encyclopedias, dictionaries, dishes, vacuum cleaners, and, of course, mattresses. Manou couldn't apply for teaching jobs because of the conundrum faced by many immigrants—she couldn't get a work permit without a job, and she couldn't get a job with her temporary student visa. Ernst had a renewable visa and wasn't under so much pressure. But hating life with the Lawry's made him equally impatient to get different work.

One evening, Edith was in bed and Jack was out so Manou and Ernst sat in the parlor away from the oppressive heat of their bedroom. Jack suddenly barged in the door, drunk. The former marine often drank himself into staggering oblivion on the weekend but tonight his lower lip was bleeding heavily. "I was kidnapped, by a fat son-of-a-bitch who beat the crap outa me. Jus' look at my face!" he wailed.

Manou could smell his fetid whiskey breath across the room. "Why did he beat you up?" asked Ernst as he and Manou stood up to leave the parlor.

Jack threw a limp arm around him, holding him in the room. "You're like a son to me. You gotta help."

Ernst removed Jack's arm from his shoulder and asked, "How can I possibly help you?"

"I got lead pipes. I got knives. Let's go. We'll beat up the son of a bitch. He's at that stink-hole bar called Tony's. Let's get 'im good." Jack stumbled around the room, flailing his arms like a shadow boxer.

"I can't do that, Jack. You've got to call the police."

Jack dropped his arms and fell into an armchair, mumbling, "So you won't help an old man?" He yanked a pint of whiskey from his back pocket and swilled the last ounce. Swinging the empty bottle in a dismissive wave, he said, "Aw, jus' call the cops."

Edith hovered in the door to the parlor with a sour expression and her arms crossed. Manou called the police while Jack alternately berated Ernst for letting him down and himself for not beating up the guy. When the policeman arrived, he asked Jack some questions and got incoherent answers about a girl and revenge. So the officer asked Edith, "Do you know what he's talking about?"

She straightened her back and lifted her chin. "I know all about that whore. Jack, you bastard, you been cheatin' on me. I gave that guy ten bucks to teach you and her a lesson."

Jack looked at her through bloodshot eyes, too drunk to grasp to her sense of betrayal.

Ernst and Manou quietly went upstairs, leaving the officer to deal with their landlords' domestic mess. Manou circled the tiny room, pressing her hands against her sweaty, throbbing temples and muttering, "*Ces personnes sont complètement folles.* They are completely crazy. We've got to get out of here."

Picking up the newspaper from the dresser, Ernst showed her a classified ad he had circled and announced, "Look, there's a job for an elevator operator at the First City Bank."

Manou stopped her pacing. "Do you think you can get this one?"

"Maybe but it says, 'Appropriate attire required.' I'll need to show up in a suit."

"But we don't have any money to get clothes," Manou answered in desperation.

"I know," Ernst replied, staring over her shoulder. At first she thought he was just retreating into himself the way he did so often these days, but when she followed his gaze she saw he was staring at his violin case propped under the windowsill.

"No, Ernst. Not that," she said, touching his cheek. Despite his fatigue and discouragement, he had practiced at least once every day, his deft fingers on the strings filling the space with a melodic elixir. It was an evening rite that comforted them both. Manou understood that selling the violin would be a deeply sacrificial act for Ernst.

"It's the only way. I'm not such a prodigy anyway."

"Oh, Ernst, you are," she answered, her eyes filling with tears. "Your playing is the one thing that keeps us going. It's your voice; it's my comfort."

"That won't feed our stomachs, though." He shrugged in resignation. "Or get us out of here."

She grabbed his shoulders. "Only if you promise that as soon as we have some money you'll get your violin back from the pawnshop."

"Perhaps."

She gave him a shake. "Not perhaps. *Yes.*"

He looked at her with puzzlement. "It is that important to you?" Manou nodded. "Then, yes, I'll get it back."

The next morning they walked ceremoniously to the pawnbroker, with Ernst cradling his instrument case as if holding a child's casket in a funeral procession. After they exchanged the instrument for a suit pawned by some other man down on his luck, Ernst went to the job interview looking extraordinarily handsome in a linen jacket and pants, a white shirt, and a navy blue tie. He lied, telling the manager he had had experience working a hospital elevator. He got the job. Ernst started the next day, dressed in uniform: red-striped pants and matching jacket, and a gray shirt with a red tie.

"It's rather festive," Manou remarked, "more like a circus uniform than that of a bank employee."

Ernst hooked his fingers in his lapels. "When I was a little boy, I wanted to play fiddle with the Italian circus. I can at least look the part now."

Manou laughed. "I never knew that about you."

"I am a man of many faces, my love. And now I will become an expert in elevator technology."

Every evening of his first week, he related the day's comedy of errors to Manou. He had to stop the elevator at exactly floor level, which he missed more often than not. Sometimes he started to close the doors too soon, catching a skirt or a briefcase between the metal grate doors. By the end of a week, though, he was a capable operator with his first paycheck in his pocket.

Within two weeks, he retrieved his violin from the pawnbroker and practiced every evening before changing out of his clownish uniform. Manou, delighted at the return of his lighthearted side, began to feel hopeful again about their future in California, but she hated doing the Lawry's endless daily chores while waiting for Ernst's return. The increasingly dour Edith seemed to relish giving her particularly nasty tasks like cleaning under sinks and scouring the garbage bins. As she dumped the fetid gray wash water on the bushes, she mumbled, "*Merde*, I have a university education and I'm throwing slop on the sumac." She stood up straight, pushed damp black strands of hair off her forehead, and resolved to get herself a real job, too. She answered a classified seeking a maid in a hotel for retired people in nearby Santa Monica, knowing that cleaning bathrooms and changing beds would be a breeze compared to endlessly patching the crumbling cottages in South LA. The manager was a kind older woman tired of surly teenage housekeepers and, in spite of Manou's visa problems, offered her and Ernst a room and three cafeteria meals a day in exchange for her services. Manou skipped with joy as she left the charming two-story building surrounded by palm trees. Now they could move out of Jack and Edith's dreadful house and break free of their clutches.

At dinner, Ernst and Manou returned the wedding rings to Jack, explaining, "We have to move on now."

Edith looked crestfallen. "But we've treated you like our own."

"I'm sorry," Manou said. "We must go. We have other work..."

"I don't think so." Jack stood up, knocking over his coffee. "I swear I'll call immigration if you leave us in the lurch."

"Do what you must," Ernst replied with a dignified shrug. He took Manou's hand and they climbed the stairs to their room.

Jack hollered after them, "How'll we keep up the cabins? You ungrateful Krauts!"

After they heard Jack slam the door on his way to the bar and Edith close her bedroom door, the young couple tiptoed out with two small suitcases, a violin, and a huge sense of relief.

Manou was the best maid the hotel had hired in years, her employer said. She quickly learned the residents' habits, interests, and quirks. A Swedish lady gave her advice on birth control, exercise, and homeopathy. An old gentleman on the second floor at the end of the hall tried to grab her breasts. She got a fifty-cent tip from a tidy lady who wanted her toilet scrubbed extra clean. Life as a chambermaid was not so bad. She worked fast and was always done by 2:00 p.m., after which she walked to the Santa Monica pier and indulged in a ten-cent ice cream cone.

Ernst, too, was well liked at his new job. In fact, his boss at the bank gave him a raise the first week of September. To celebrate their good fortune, Ernst and Manou took a day off and caught the bus to Hermosa Beach. There they watched little crabs tickle their feet and swam in the waves pounding the shore. That night they made love and felt closer than they had in months.

Two days later, the sky fell. They picked up their mail at the post office general delivery counter and found a letter to Ernst from the U.S. Army draft board. He was eligible for the draft because he was no longer a student, and the letter said he either had to go back to Europe or report in three weeks to Fort Ord at Monterey Bay, near San Francisco. If he served in the US Army, he would qualify for citizenship. Further complicating matters, Manou's student visa was due to expire about the same time.

Manou was incredulous. Having finally come to believe they were going to make it work in California, she found the thought of being separated unbearable. While she fought back endless tears, Ernst dove into a brooding impenetrable silence.

Worse, they had to make their decisions quickly. They went over their choices again and again. Manou didn't want to stay in LA without Ernst, and lacking a formal job, she couldn't apply for a work permit. Her scholarship fund would pay for her to return to France from Iowa City, but she needed thirty-five dollars for the bus ticket to get there, no small amount in their situation. They thought briefly of going to Canada to escape the draft, but that was impossible, given their financial situation. Furthermore, Ernst did not relish the idea of forever being a fugitive. He liked the idea of becoming an American citizen. They came to the inescapable conclusion that Ernst would go to Fort Ord, and Manou would go back to France.

They lay in their small room at the retirees' hotel, barely touching in their misery. Manou whispered, so softly Ernst could hardly hear her, "Perhaps we could get married before we separate? Wouldn't it make things easier?"

Ernst scowled slightly.

Manou turned to the wall and feigned sleep, afraid to find out what he really thought about the idea. Her parents' diatribe about Hitler came rushing back, as did his father's litany of Napoleonic crimes against Deutschland. Perhaps it was a union not meant to be, she thought, and didn't mention marriage again.

Ernst gave notice at the bank. His manager was proud that Ernst was going into the U.S. Army and wrote him an excellent recommendation. One morning Ernst told Manou he wasn't going to work that day, and she should put on a nice dress. They were going to city hall to get a marriage license. She was thrilled but looked down and said shyly, "Yes, Ernst, I love you so much." His decision was the last word.

At the county clerk's office, at least thirty couples waited in front of them. Most were dressed up, in preparation for their complementary photograph. The room was stifling and noisy. The muscles along Ernst's jaw flexed, and Manou, now able to recognize little clues to his moods, knew he was getting upset, so she linked arms with him, hoping to cheer him up.

When they finally got to the window, the clerk unceremoniously handed them a form to fill out and a sheet of printed directions. As they read the instructions, Ernst and Manou realized they needed a blood test and would have to make a doctor's appointment, pay for the test, and wait a week for the results. Since Ernst was due at Fort Ord in two weeks and they had neither the time nor the money to complete the application procedure, they agreed that the form would have to serve for now as a document signifying their commitment to each other. They also agreed that Manou should go back to France as planned. Ernst reassured her that they would get married eventually, and when Manou saw his face relax, she knew he was relieved.

They spent their last day together at the beach, but their hearts weren't in it. They languished on the sand then went back to the hotel and made frantic, sad love all night. Before dawn, Manou confessed she was afraid she would never see Ernst again. To console her, he told her he had a special surprise for her that would convince her beyond a doubt of his love for her.

Manou spent the last morning packing, and then she caught a city bus to the Greyhound station, where Ernst planned to meet her during his lunch break from the bank. Ernst was waiting on the curb in front of the terminal with his violin on his shoulder, wearing his red-and-white striped uniform, playing the Corrente, the festive second movement of Bach's Partita II. He followed her to the ticket counter like a circus musician, moving with the little running steps of the traditional Italian dance. Ernst smiled his gloriously beautiful smile and his blond locks fell over his forehead. The other passengers grinned and clapped along. "I'll see you in Paris as soon as possible!" were his last words as she boarded the bus. For Manou his performance was so enchanting and bittersweet that after boarding the bus, she cried from Los Angeles to Albuquerque. In southern Colorado, she stared in misery at the incredible landscape that reminded her of their wondrous journey west in the black LaSalle.

Crossing the southern Rockies during the night, the bus got chilly, and she ached for Ernst's warmth. Outside Denver, her back began to hurt, and she alternately wept, vomited, and slept the rest of the way across the plains. By the time she reached Iowa City, she knew that she was pregnant.

Sarabanda

The Slow Dance

For a few months after Ernst's death, Manou persuaded herself that life was going on as before in spite of his absence. Because of the newspaper accounts, the kids' classmates weren't as kind as she thought they would be. They had asked them a lot of blunt, disturbing questions like, "What was wrong with your dad?" "Why couldn't he drive right? My mom said he was drunk." "How come your dad killed himself?" Francis and Florence came home crying at least once a week. Karl remained a stoic and Sophia copied him, but they finally admitted it bothered them, too.

On Dr. Tremont's suggestion, Manou took them to a psychiatrist recommended by Dr. Tremont. The doctor was an older man, with a shock of white hair and a cane. He had penetrating but kind dark eyes. He sat all five of them down in his office and gently explained to the children what happened the day of their father's death. "Your father went to see Dr. Campbell," Dr. Elliot said. "He was very tired, mentally tired. Do you know what that means?" Sophia nodded. The little ones listened to his soothing voice but just wiggled their legs against the sofa. Karl said nothing. The doctor continued, "He was so upset that it affected his driving. Whatever else people say, I'm sure he had an accident." Manou watched her children's faces visibly relax as though that simple declaration that it was an accident gave them the tool they needed to answer classmates' questions and calm their inner fears about why Ernst was gone. The doctor added, "And I know he loved you very much."

When they left the office, Manou commented, "He was a nice man, wasn't he?"

Francis and Florence nodded vigorously and ran ahead. Karl and Sophia exchanged a silent glance.

"Would it be helpful for you to see him again?" Manou asked them.

Sophia shrugged with indifference.

"No. It's okay. I just want to get home," Karl stated with an abrupt nod.

Manou sighed. "All right then. We're fine." We'll try the old Méthode Coué, she told herself. "We're fine," she repeated to Sophia and Karl.

They didn't go back to the psychiatrist. Manou desperately wanted to get on with family life so they settled back in their routines. The cloud of his absence hovered over them, though, so she took them to Disneyland for Easter in a brand-new Buick station wagon that she had bought with some of Ernst's car insurance money. Whether it was the larger than life Mickey Mouse or the sun that sprinkled their cheeks with freckles, the kids cheered up. She also supervised the construction of the swimming pool Ernst had promised the kids when they moved to Walnut Creek. Manou kept busy, distracted by teaching, the kids, and wrangling with the finances. Against her will, she was a capable head of household.

Summer arrived, foggy along the coast, but hot at their house in the foothills of Mount Diablo. The new swimming pool was perfect for the kids to cool down at any time. They had friends over every day and ate outdoors on the patio. Manou settled in for her vacation from teaching and Maman came for a month. It was her first visit to the United States and they spent leisurely days together sunbathing on the lawn and supervising the kids. Maman was gentler as a grandmother than she had been as a mother. Manou realized she often used her mother's directive style in her own response to whining kids. Raising four children over the years made her understand that order was essential if a woman was to carve a life of her own out of the constant willful chaos of family. Manou's resentment of her mother's tough parenting mellowed, and this summer especially, Manou welcomed Maman's orderly ministrations to her brood and the positive affirmations of the Méthode Coué.

Nonetheless, Manou would not risk telling her mother how she felt every night in the privacy of her room. She ached not so much for the resentful man of the last couple of years of their marriage but for the young man she had missed so deeply on that lonely bus ride back to Iowa. Maman surely would tell her—and she told herself—you can make it on your own. Life goes on. Life goes on.

One steamy afternoon while Maman napped, Manou watched as Francis and Sophia frolicked in the water. Sophia called to her brother, "I bet I can stay underwater longer than you can!"

"Bet you can't," he yelled back. "Dad taught me how to stay under a long time." They lined up against the edge of the pool in the shallow end. They dunked under and pushed off. Manou watched their lithe bodies pull and kick through the blue water. Halfway down the pool Francis burst to the surface gasping and splashing. He took a deep breath then dunked back under and swam farther as Sophia popped her head up and huffed and puffed until her lungs were full again. She arched like a fish and dove under. They forgot the challenge and just kept swimming laps underwater, surfacing in loud bubbles and laughs, and then plunging in again. As their game went on, Manou felt a slow rush of adrenaline spread through her body. A scene flooded her memory with such clarity that she laid back on a lounge chair, the sounds of the kids a distant backdrop.

Manou stared at the mountain, tried to refuse the memory with all her emotional strength, but it was there, as undeniable and instantaneous as a tremor along the San Andreas Fault. She and Ernst were in the Pleasant Hill house three years earlier. They were in the bathroom where she was collecting laundry from the hamper. He was in the tub, lying completely flat underwater and practicing holding his breath. He asked her to time how long he could stay under. He took a noisy gulp of air, went under, and she checked her watch. His blond hair waved slightly around his open eyes. He had gained weight over the last few years and exercised infrequently. Underwater, he looked strangely pale, like wet, white clay. She glanced back and forth from him to her watch. One minute, two minutes, three minutes. He just stared at her from underwater. His eyes looked like pockets of blue water inside the clay. After another half minute, she reached into the tub and shook him. "Ernst, stop it!" she protested as he slid to the surface and blew out a long slow breath. "This isn't youth camp. It's frightening."

"There comes a point when it is pleasurable, really. It's kind of intoxicating, especially when you practice." He looked past her with a remote gaze and added, as if speaking to the wall behind her, "But you know that, don't you?"

"I do not know that. It's too strange."

Ernst darted his eyes back to her face, a little surprised, as if her presence was unexpected and unwelcome. "What?"

"Promise me you won't scare me like that again?"

He sank down into the tub with his face just above the surface. "All right, I won't."

From the pool, Sophia called her to throw them the ball that was beside her chair. Manou snapped her eyes open, not even realizing that she had closed them. The bathroom scene vanished. Manou shook away the memory and pushed his shadow back one more time. She grabbed the colorful beach ball, jumped in the pool, and tossed it to her daughter. So often the life force of a child had saved her from collapse, beginning with her first pregnancy, when Ernst was a different kind of shadow, thousands of miles across the Atlantic.

♪

Those were the heroic days when travelers crossed the ocean by ship, knowing the Cold War simmered between the Soviet Union and the United States; the civilized days when first-class stewards still served three-course meals under a swaying chandelier and gentlemen set their watches one hour ahead each day, gently getting used to the time change; the brave days when passengers walked the decks or lay in lounge chairs under wool blankets getting lashed with driving rain or sea spray against the hull. Manou sailed back to France in October 1953, as she had sailed to the United States a year before, spending most of her time in her stateroom. On this voyage, it wasn't seasickness that kept her confined; it was classic morning sickness.

Marie Madeleine felt neither courageous nor genteel nor adventuresome, as she lay curled in her berth wrestling with her stomach and with her loss. She had told Ernst about the pregnancy but he had responded with neither shock nor enthusiasm. It was hard to decipher his tone on a scratchy long distant call. He simply promised he would come to see her as soon as possible. Manou lay in the poorly lit room and longed for Ernst's love, their mutual quest, and their idealism. Those things had made her flow with *élan vital* in spite of the struggles of life in Los Angeles. She yearned for Ernst Fiedler, that extraordinary man who became more handsome, more talented, and more essential to her happiness as North America disappeared on the horizon. On the other hand, to the east were her parents, her childhood, *son identité française.* Her spirit floated between the two shores, rocking back and forth, like the new life force within her.

The boat docked in Le Havre. As the sailors were lashing the giant ropes to the cleats, Manou saw her parents' wave from shore. They looked just the same and it surprised her. Manou felt as she'd been gone a decade instead of less than a year. What did I expect? I have changed, not them, Manou told herself. When she arrived at the terminal they hugged her and kissed her on each cheek, and Papa went to find her luggage. Maman held her at arms length and looked Manou up and down. With a little frown at her daughter's threadbare cotton blouse and plaid skirt, she exclaimed, "*Mon Dieu*, what are you wearing. You look so, so *américaine*."

"Oh, Maman, really I just..."

"And where is your wedding ring? What kind of husband is this who sends you off without a ring?"

Manou winced, uncomfortable with the lie about marrying Ernst that she had put in a telegram from Iowa City. "We didn't have much money, just enough to get me home."

"Ah, in that case, we can make an exception." And Maman nudged her through the disembarking crowds to follow Papa.

Manou felt a flood of resentment. Maman would never understand how her experience had enlarged her life, opened her eyes to the world. All she cared about was a silly ring and clothes. Not ten minutes in France and Manou felt like a scolded child again. It was the Old World that she and Ernst each had so desperately escaped. There was no way she could tell them that she and Ernst weren't even married yet, especially with the news Manou must break as soon as possible.

"Maman, stop a minute."

"But Marie Madeleine, we have to find your father and get in the car. The Rue George V is a horror of traffic ..."

Manou clutched her mother's coat. "Arrête! I think I am pregnant."

Maman faced her in stunned silence; a shocked look crossed her face that she shed as fast as it appeared. She clasped her hands tightly together and then abruptly unclasped them. "We can take care of you. We can. Until Ernst comes to get you. We can. Now, we need to find your father. Follow me." Maman walked toward the baggage claim with a stiff back.

Manou sighed and followed her. She knew that gesture of the Méthode Coué so well. Clasp the hands as if you can't let go, and then open them and you are back in control. Maman would rise to the occasion as always. This was nothing compared to a war, after all. Manou followed her feeling like a poor weak bird that had tried to fly too soon. Her parents were picking her up and carrying her back to the nest. Her need for them was both humiliating and comforting.

Although Manou had been unable to eat much on the ship, the simple French food served at her parents' table reawakened her appetite. Fresh vegetables and seafood, dishes that took hours to fix like quenelles, chicken liver soufflés, ratatouilles, bouillabaisse, fancy desserts, and good wine brought up from the cellar. After Wonder Bread and jelly sandwiches, the French baguette was mouth-watering. And her pleasure drinking that big cup of café au lait every morning was almost sinful.

After a few days, though, the pleasure of French ways began to settle into the doldrums of old habits. Maman and Papa never varied in their routine. Papa went to work at the Berliet dealership that had sold and serviced trucks for decades, even German trucks during the occupation. Maman did her shopping and kept the house looking exactly the same as it had when Manou left for America, down to the position of mementos and sepia photos of ancestors on the side tables, the thick, dull drapes locking out the day, and dark and still oil paintings on the few square centimeters of wall space. Manou began to feel claustrophobic, and intensely irritated every time Maman clasped and unclasped her hands in her gesture of coping with something she didn't agree with or understand. The fireplaces were never lit and everything recalled the dreary war years. Only mealtimes brought back memories of effervescent family gatherings. Otherwise a light was missing in her parents' home, yes, ordinary light—California sunshine. Although, she admitted, perhaps the missing glow was Ernst's blonde hair and blazing eyes.

One morning at breakfast, Papa pushed a small box across the table. "Here. This is for you until your husband buys you a nice one." It was a gold plated wedding ring. Manou almost laughed since it was so like the one Edith and Jack had given them.

"It is important," snapped Maman, her lips turning down at Manou's apparent amusement, "especially in your condition."

Manou ran upstairs before she cried at the implied judgment of Ernst but mostly because it also made her remember them standing for hours at the county offices waiting to get married only to be turned away with the infuriating forms and applications. But Manou was her mother's daughter, well schooled in facing reality, so she stopped her sobbing, rinsed her face with cold water, and returned to the table. She took the ring out of the box, jammed it on her ring finger, and with a defiant look at her father and mother, said, "C'est mieux, hein?" Better, don't you think?

They both nodded solemnly.

Manou was in a no man's land, not belonging anywhere, not at Ernst's boot camp nor her family home. In Nantes, she seemed to be playing the little girl still looking for approval and care, and then resenting it bitterly. She would lie in bed at night, unable to sleep even under the thick down coverlet, remembering why America had offered her such a sense of liberation from the naughty girl image steadfastly held by her mother and father. She recalled one of her first memories of being on a train with her mother. Little Manou chatted and danced and sang to the other people in their compartment, and they cheered her gregarious performances. Suddenly Maman pulled her aside and hissed furiously, "Arrête, Marie Madeleine! You are showing off. Ça suffit."

On the other hand, Maman's immovable resolve and implacability had gotten them through the privations of war. Every day she walked into town in a threadbare wool coat, her hair wound in two tight braids on her head, her chin up. She queued up at various stores to get rations. Although she had a priority card so she could feed her children, she often had to elbow for her place in line. But she always brought something home, even if it was only fish and rutabagas. Manou had never seen her mother linger in bed except when her sister was born. She got up before everyone else in the morning, partly because Papa had intractable habits, but mostly because she drove herself harder than she drove anyone else. There was no flexibility in their routine. Everything had to be exactly on time. The hour is the hour, or "*L'heure c'est l'heure*," Papa yelled if he didn't get exactly what he wanted when he wanted it. He took after his own mother who was unbearably bossy and irritable. If Manou was grumpy, Maman said, "You have a nasty disposition just like your grand-mère." This infuriated Manou who detested her ill-tempered, skinny Grand-mère as much as she recoiled every time her Papa started tapping his watch.

While Papa was militaristic in his commands, Maman could put anyone down, including the patriarch of the house. When Manou and her sister Odette were little, Maman and Papa would have loud, long arguments full of blame and invectives that shook the windows and rattled the doors like a squall blowing in from the sea. Maman would finally get up, put on her hat and coat, and say, "Alright, that's enough. I'm putting on my hat and I'm getting out of here." She paused on the threshold with a ferocious look, then walked out and stayed away for ten unbearable minutes. Manou and Odette cowered under the kitchen table, afraid of Papa's anger and terrified that Maman would never return. Yet invariably Papa settled down, Maman walked back in, and everything went back to a tight, hushed control.

The girls were unnerved at Maman's melodramatic departures because, while Maman ruled over Papa, he ruled over his girls with relentless judgment. When Manou was in elementary school, a private Catholic school, the nuns ranked students each week. The best students were given a decoration, and Manou proudly took an Honor cross with a blue ribbon home to show her father. He thrust the little pendant back at her, snorted, and said, "*Ce n'est pas assez bien.* You should have gotten the Excellence cross not just the Honor."

Odette never invited as much parental exasperation as Manou did. It was in Odette's quiet nature to behave. "Manou, be like your sister Odette," Maman demanded. "She is so good. Play quietly with her for a change."

Years later Odette scoffed, "Yes, they always called me good Odette, poor Odette. Which label do you think is hardest to get rid of, Manou? Poor girl or bad girl?"

The message was decidedly mixed. When Manou was caught in a transgression, Maman looked over her severe thin nose and declared, "You are forever the bad girl." Then she sighed and shrugged. "Yes, but you are the bad girl who will always manage." It was worse than simply being scolded. Back in her childhood bed, Manou awoke every morning as she did when she was a girl, infused with anxiety about what veiled criticism her mother or father might level at her between breakfast and bedtime, and worse, whether to be proud or ashamed of their disapproval.

Luckily, the university soon contacted her to tell her she needed to finish her last semester in Paris to complete her Physical Education degree, so at first she gladly moved away from Nantes for a few months. Yet Paris was lonely. Ernst didn't write very often and Manou didn't socialize much because of her pregnancy. Her mind was far from school, far from Paris, and far from her family; it swam with the unborn child in her womb over the vast Atlantic and flew across the American continent to Fort Ord in California. She sometimes imagined a bridge between her and their infant all the way to Ernst at the army boot camp, and she crossed it with the words she wrote in letters every night. *Good evening, my love,* she wrote in her tiny student room, *Would you like to take a walk with me this evening? I feel like walking, holding your hand, saying nothing. I only want to feel you next to me in the cool evening air. How I dream, how I call for you, how I wait for you with all my strength. But I know you wouldn't like me to be sad, so I am not sad. I try to forget myself, my discomfort. I want you to know you can rely on me.*

Manou completed her semester by Christmas, but then she had to decide where to spend the last four months of her pregnancy. Maman and Papa were so dismal she simply couldn't imagine going back to them. Aunt Marraine came to the rescue by inviting her to share her apartment in Lyon. "I am a widow, now, a bit lonely. Why don't you give me your company for a few months, Manou?" Marraine wrote her. Manou jumped at the opportunity. Her godmother was the saving grace of her family and had always treated Manou like an individual, never embarrassing her or making insidious comments, simply accepting Manou for herself. So often in her childhood, Manou had wished Marraine were her mother. She was a beautiful woman with dark hair and a lovely cheerful face. She smelled of rose water and glycerin and wore gorgeous understated clothes of soft wool or shimmering silk. Marraine had a collection of charming hats that she made herself when she worked as a milliner. Maman was very bitter because, when Manou was growing up, Marraine's lover, an older man who eventually married her, supported her. Mother said, "She is lucky; *she* doesn't have to work anymore."

By the time Manou returned from America, her aunt lived alone in a charming apartment. From the soft mossy stone at the entrance to the ancient tapestries on the walls, the place possessed natural elegance coupled with artistic style. The antique furniture nestled against ceiling to floor velvet drapes. Old porcelain figurines danced on the chests. In the tiny bathroom, perfumed soaps nested in rose-colored glass bowls and cologne water filled a Lalique crystal bottle. And Marraine threw open the curtains every morning to invite in light.

After Manou moved in with Marraine, it was as if a shroud slipped from her shoulders and she could live in ease again. Marraine fed her culinary miracles at the kitchen table, embraced her often and spontaneously, and let her settle into a long quiet winter gestation.

One evening as they sat in the parlor knitting, Marraine asked, "So what is this man of yours like?"

Manou smiled. No other member of her family had bothered to ask, but had only made side comments about him being German. "Oh, Marraine, he is so elegant. So handsome in that Wagnerian way. Blonde, strong, tall..."

"Yes, *chérie*, that tells me that he is probably a wonderful lover but what is he *like?*"

Manou had to think how to answer. "Ernst is a little enigmatic. He is a violinist, you know. This is his passion and his true self comes out when he is playing more than when he speaks."

"Men can be so terribly uncommunicative, can't they, but then suddenly fall apart like little boys."

"So often I just can't tell what he's thinking. He goes behind a very dark cloud. To be honest it scares me sometimes."

Marraine nodded. "It can be wise to be scared." She put down her knitting. "He has never hit you has he?"

"Oh, *Mon Dieu*, no. It is more that he just disappears behind his eyes. I can't find him until he is ready."

Marraine reached over and gave her hand a squeeze. "Men are all the same but when you have a special one, you hang on. *C'est vrai?* Right?"

"Can I tell you something I haven't told my parents?"

Marraine laughed. "I suspect there are a lot of things you don't tell those parents of yours. Sometimes I think they are still living in the 1930s when life was so predictable...and very controlled, especially for us women. So, what is your little secret? I'm sorry to say but we already know you are pregnant." She patted Manou's swollen belly.

Manou gave her a playful swat. "My secret is that Ernst and I weren't able to get married. We tried but we needed too many forms and we didn't have any money for a blood test and we ran out of time..."

Marraine shrugged. "You know I was Jean Claude's lover for many years before we married, so who am I to judge."

"I knew that." He was married to another woman, and it wasn't a family secret; it was more like a mild annoyance to Maman.

"He loved me very much but his wife was in a sanatorium for years and he felt he couldn't leave her. When she died, he married me right away. Ah, Manou, he treated me well." Marraine closed her eyes and put her head back on the sofa. Then she opened one eye mischievously. "Your mother was so jealous because he bought me ermine scarves and silk stockings. Such luxury for a short time!"

"But didn't he leave you some money?"

"He left most of it to his useless son who gambled it away in Monaco. Such is life, Manou, and as a woman, you must always have something to fall back on if your man fails you. At least I have a little pension and these nice things."

"But Ernst will marry me."

"I have no doubt. Just don't rely on him entirely. If we learned anything during the war it is that life is short and unpredictable."

"I understand. I didn't get an education for nothing." Manou suddenly felt tired, as she often did in this last trimester of her pregnancy. She sighed and snuggled into the cushions. "Marraine, tell me that story you used to tell me at grandmother's house in the summer."

"Which one?"

"Our favorite, about the goat."

"Oh, you mean *Monsieur Seguin's Goat.* But it used to make you cry."

"Yes, but we loved it. Go ahead."

"Monsieur Seguin had terrible luck keeping his goats. One after another, they ran away into the mountains and got eaten by a wolf. One day Mr. Seguin got a very special little kid and was determined to protect her forever..." And Marraine told the story with all the dramatic inflection that had entranced Manou and her cousins. But Manou fell asleep with her head curled on her hands before hearing the gruesome demise of the cherished goat at the end of the story.

Over the long winter, Manou kept her restless mind active by studying German with *Assimil*, a language learning system which involved listening to records and reading a book with the same text, one side French, one side German. Manou hoped it would better prepare her for speaking Ernst's language than the old school grammatical method of learning English that had left her so lost when she got to New York. She would listen at night, sleep on it, and then write everything she remembered the next morning and begin a new lesson. In one of his rare letters, Ernst wrote that he was intrigued by the system she described because he was beginning to teach German to other recruits at Fort Ord.

During the day, she meandered about in a semi-vegetative state, with Marraine's full approval. She knitted baby clothes, walked around the neighborhood, went to a weekly movie, checked the mail for the infrequent letter from Ernst, and wrote to him.

Today, my darling, I was looking at your picture, trying to engrave each trait of your face within myself so as to imprint our child with them. It would be so wonderful if he resembles you. You probably think I am silly to spend hours looking at your picture but, no, I am simply in love, more than ever. You see, I talk to you, question you, scold you sometimes. I kiss you. I think I could read the answers in your smile, this little smile of yours, ironic and tender at the same time.

As her belly grew, the three flights of stairs to Marraine's apartment took more and more effort. She soon finished the whole *Assimil* course in German and had a basket full of baby blankets and socks and caps and sweaters. One afternoon in early April, she wrote Ernst, *Tell me we'll be together soon. I am bored here. It is so monotonous. Truly, I couldn't live in Europe anymore...* She felt a cramp and shifted position at the antique desk. She missed her lithe body, running and swimming and climbing. *Are you still swimming in the ocean? Do you remember the day we were looking for crabs with a fork and we buried the fork for the next time we came to the beach? Right by the little tree, the third one from the playground. We could find it again, I am sure...* Again the cramp. She had been having light false labor contractions for several months so she stretched and rubbed her belly and said, "Hush, child. Let me write." *My darling, come sleep with me. I feel like snuggling up. Tender kisses...* And the cramp grabbed her abdomen with a vengeance. Manou gasped. "Marraine! *Il vient!*"

Marraine ran into her room, settled her on the bed, stroked her forehead, and calmed her as the contractions came again and again. "Okay, they seem very regular. I'll get a cab and call the doctor and your mother and father."

Soon they carefully stepped down the three flights of stairs to the street and into a waiting cab. At the hospital, the birth was quick, and beautiful Karl burst into the doctor's waiting hands with a robust cry. Maman sent a telegram to Ernst and he telegrammed back the next day that he had gotten a two-week leave and would arrive in Lyon in late May. The French hospital was solicitous of new mothers and wouldn't allow Manou to sit up for four days, and then she had to stay in bed for one week, gradually standing and walking the corridors of the maternity ward. The baby, wearing the little outfits she had knitted, was adored by everyone, and Manou had never seen such tender smiles on her parents' faces.

When she left the hospital the whole family went to La Bâtie in the southern Alps near Grenoble. Before the war, Marraine had bought the lovely old country place for their parents. She felt they deserved something special because they had worked so hard all of their lives, Grand-père, Pépé, as a foundry worker and Grand-mère, Mémé, as a textile worker. La Bâtie was a very tiny village on the side of the mountains, compact and pretty, too small even to have a center square. The big old house sat in a valley outside of town. It had many rooms so relatives came and went all summer. Only the kitchen had running water so everyone enjoyed a rustic life, using an outhouse, carrying hot water from the kitchen in buckets for baths, and using a chamber pot at night. Manou noticed with her new American eyes that Mémé, Maman, Odette and the other aunts and cousins did all the work, quibbling in the kitchen, preparing meals, while Pépé tended the vegetable garden.

Papa, Odette's husband Pierre, uncles, and nephews were treated like kings when they would come for weekends from Lyon, Nantes, or Paris. They did nothing all day except perhaps kill a chicken from the coop or a rabbit from the hutch with great bravado. Every evening the women would complain about doing all the cooking and cleaning, and then they would get up the next day and do it again.

In La Bâtie, the children were like horses let out of the barn. It had been paradise for Manou as a little *garçon manqué*, a tomboy racing through the fields, climbing trees, and directing her siblings and cousins in plays they performed in costumes exhumed from the attic—dresses, capes, ankle boots, moth-eaten furs, and corsets. Manou realized she visualized her childhood in Nantes and Lyon and Quimper in black and white, but every memory of summer at La Bâtie was in full color. She was thrilled her son could spend his first month in the place she loved most.

Karl cried in the middle of the first night but Mémé always had little remedies. She loved to solve others' ailments, and if no one was sick, she'd find plenty of her own to complain about. Mémé told Manou that Karl was colicky, brewed her some anise tea, and told her to nurse the baby. He settled down happily at Manou's breast, staring up at the solicitous old woman.

Maman stood in the doorway with a scowl and said, "Don't coddle him. You have to let him cry or he'll be up all night."

A few days later, he developed a little cough and Mémé brought in a steaming kettle of water with camphor. She was so different from Maman who held everyone to the standards of the Méthode Coué, without which you would succumb to "the tolling of St. John's bell" that mourned the dead. Maman said, "Remember Great Aunt Clotilde who had crippling arthritis. St. John's bell had rung for her," meaning she'd done something bad that none of Mémé's remedies had ever worked.

Manou shivered remembering how terrified she and Odette and their cousins always were that St. John's bell might ring for them and punish them if they made a nasty face or lied or did something forbidden. Manou learned to make compromises in her head that allowed her to be herself while fitting into Maman's regimented codes. As a child, she'd clean her room perfectly then go run on roofs with the boys. As a teen, she'd get good grades but invent sins to shock the priest in confession. She went to the university but studied in America with the ones who had bombed Nantes to rubble at the end of the war. From school she had slipped away to California to live with her lover, a German, no less.

Her German sweetheart arrived exhausted, disheveled, emaciated, and empty-handed at the end of May 1954. Ernst had hitchhiked on planes from one airbase to another for seventy-two hours until he reached the Paris-Orly airport. He then hopped a train to Lyon for free because his French was so flawless the ticket collectors thought he was a French soldier.

He hadn't changed his clothes once during the entire trip so Maman was not impressed. "Where is his suitcase? Is a he a *voyageur sans baggage*, a bum?"

"*Pardonnez-moi, Madame. Je vous prie de pardonner mon aspect terrible.* I am just a lowly soldier who wants to see his son and his wife." He smiled his most warm and charming smile, and Maman melted in spite of herself.

"Oh, I suppose we can find you some clean clothes."

Manou led him upstairs to her room and, as soon as the door was closed, they embraced and kissed, feeling all of the charge of their first attraction. When they finally let go, Ernst picked up Karl and rocked his son gently. Karl gurgled and swatted his papa's gaunt cheeks.

Manou looked at him carefully. He had dark circles and bags under his eyes, which seemed larger than normal in his drawn face. His body did not look robust and athletic. Ernst caught her concerned gaze. "I haven't been well," he admitted.

"What's wrong, my love?"

"I have problems with my thyroid. The ocean air and seawater at Fort Ord knocked my iodine out of balance and I get rashes and heart palpitations. That's why I've lost weight."

" *C'est terrible, mon chéri.*"

"They wanted me to go in the hospital in California but I told them I had to come here. To be with you."

She hugged him close. "Will you be all right?"

"Yes, but I have to go to the army hospital in Frankfurt for treatment as soon as possible. Will you come with me?"

"I am never letting you out of my sight again." She put Karl back in his crib and pulled Ernst down on the bed.

They spent a couple of days in Lyon. After a few glasses of wine, Papa told Ernst, "If anyone can tame our bad girl, it will surely be a German." Ernst was not offended, and he and Manou laughed in bed that night about their parents' old ideas about the German character.

With Karl bundled in one of Manou's blankets, they got on a night train across Germany to visit Ernst parents' home in Hof, near Czechoslovakia. "Keep a close eye on Marie Madeleine," advised Papa as they pulled out of the station. The exhausted Ernst slept fitfully while Manou fumed that her parents presumed she needed Ernst to take care of her. It was like sending her to school with the nuns when she was a rebellious fourteen-year-old. Now she had a child and a man yet they still treated her like she was an adolescent needing supervision. I will never live in Europe again, Manou vowed while the train sped through the night and her son nursed at her breast.

As they got off the train, Manou had her first opportunity to try out her German. She greeted Ernst's parents with *"Ich bin glücklich, hier zu sein."* I'm happy to be here. Ernst looked at her with surprise and the Feidlers smiled and welcomed her in return: *"Wir sind glücklich, daß Sie hier sind."*

Mutti welcomed Manou to Germany but her future mother-in-law didn't smile. She rocked baby Karl with warm cooing and then looked up at her son with grave concern. "You should never have left home, Ernst. They haven't taken good care of you in America. No one cares about you like your family, you know."

Walking behind his mother, Ernst rolled his eyes at Manou but said, "It was the ocean not the nation. I'll be fine, Mutti. You'll see."

Mutti cooked a traditional German dinner of sausages and cabbage that Ernst devoured and Manou nibbled at because the food tasted greasy and overcooked. A moment of nostalgia for Marraine's exquisite crepes with cream flew around her mind like the hummingbird around the geraniums on her aunt's porch. She sighed for all things French and ate to be polite. At least it wasn't as bad as American mashed potatoes and gravy. Instead of sitting with them at the table, Mutti scooped the baby out of Manou's arms. "Little Karl is too thin. He must have some *Schleim* to fatten him up," and she disappeared into the tiny kitchen.

Manou looked around at the apartment, amazed at its miniscule rooms. She turned to Ernst's father and asked, "Have you always lived here, Mr. Feidler?"

"Please call me Max."

"Yes, alright, how long has this been your home, Max?"

"We came here a year before Ernst went to America."

"And before that?"

"We lived in Plauen."

"But that is in East Germany. Did you escape?" Manou was surprised that Ernst had never mentioned this.

Mutti called out from the kitchen. "Plauen wasn't as bad as you might think. Believe me, we did not *choose* to cross those muddy fields in the middle of the night with just one suitcase holding all we owned in the world."

Max added without expression, "You see it wasn't a good thing to have a son who could speak both Russian and English—to the wrong people." Manou looked at Ernst in confusion. He just shrugged. Ernst's father coughed and his frail shoulders shook. Mutti stood in the doorway to the kitchen, her face barely illuminated in the dim light, patting Karl's tiny back methodically. A little too hard, Manou thought, so she got up to retrieve her son. "*Danke, Mutti, trage ich ihn jetzt.*" I'll carry him now. Mutti let the blanket slide through her fingers like ribbon as Manou walked back to her place at the table.

"Your German is quite good," Max said after drinking a long draught of his beer.

"German has been somewhat difficult for me to learn," Manou said, glad to change the subject and hold her warm child close again. "Some words that are feminine in French are the opposite in German. Like *die sonne* and *der mond* are *le soleil* and *la lune* in French."

Mr. Feidler smiled. "The sun must be feminine because of the heat, of course."

Manou smiled demurely, thinking Mr. Feidler was being risqué. She stole a glance at Mutti whose mouth was a tight straight line.

"Are you all done?" the dour woman said abruptly. The men pushed their empty plates back and Mutti cleared the table. Manou rose to help but Mutti waved her back with a brusque flip of her wrist.

Ernst stood and pulled Manou to her feet by her elbow. "We're going to bed now," he announced, and he guided her up the stairs to his little room under the eaves. A shelf still held all his athletic trophies for swimming, running, and fencing.

As she put the infant to bed, Manou told Ernst, "I didn't expect your parents to be so accepting. Your father even seemed to have a sense of humor. But he is so frail."

"He was taken prisoner in both wars. In England in 1917 and in Russia in 1941. Bad luck. Bad for his health."

"What did you do in the occupied territories that put your family in danger? Did it have anything to do with those tribunals about the Hitler youth you told me about?"

Ernst lay back on the makeshift bed with his arm over his eyes. He was silent so long she thought he had fallen asleep but he dropped his arm to the blanket and said, "Our parents didn't want our marriage to happen, that's for sure. But what can they do? We'll get a license back in America when I'm well." He rolled over and hugged her tightly. "We've decided, *und das ist das.*"

Manou kissed him deeply and whispered, "And *l'heure c'est l'heure, mon amour.*"

They spent two days walking around the village of Hof and had uncomfortable dinners of meat and boiled vegetables while Mutti spooned porridge into Karl's surprised lips. Mutti was so restrained and proper that at first Manou thought she must be the reason Ernst always punctuated their quarrels with a sneer about her lack of virginity. On the other hand, he thought nothing of walking around the apartment naked even in front of his mother. It struck her as so odd and unseemly but she remembered her father saying, "Although Germans and French may live very few miles apart, we are so different it might as well be different continents." At the time, she had inwardly scoffed that this merely reflected his bitterness about the wars; now she saw some truth in his perspective.

Ernst needed to check into the hospital before he was considered AWOL so they caught a train to Frankfurt. Mutti had called a friend with a home near the US Army base who graciously offered the young family a room and even wanted to baby-sit Karl.

After they settled in with Frau Koch, they went to the hospital for Ernst's diagnosis. It was not good news. He needed a thyroidectomy but couldn't have the surgery until he regained his strength. They wanted him to stay in the hospital for nutritional support and observation for two months.

It was a languid time for Ernst and Manou. Manou spent every morning with the baby and then went to the hospital in the afternoon. It was noisy and public on the ward, and they ached for some privacy. One day he impishly grabbed her hand and led her up a stairwell. She followed him in his ubiquitous blue bathrobe, complaining, "Where are you taking me. I want some more of that roast beef on your lunch tray. They feed you like a king."

"I am a king, and you must see what I've found in the castle tower." At the top of three flights of stairs, he swung open a heavy door into an attic filled with hundreds of surplus beds. They bounced from bed to bed, laughing about the creaky metal bed and horrible mattress at Jack's, kissing, and finally making love with all the lust of lovers who had been constrained by circumstance too long. All summer it was their clandestine boudoir.

In the hot sticky aftermath of their passion, Manou tried to peer inside the sphinx-like Ernst Feidler because after love he seemed a little distant yet softer and vulnerable. "Since I've been back, I've been looking at my family and how they've shaped me. It's been very interesting. Maman always says I was such a *garçon manqué*, always getting myself into trouble, climbing walls and trees with the boys."

"I was a daredevil, too. Mutti was so worried all the time for my safety that I had to go overboard for some excitement."

"What did you do?"

"I started young apparently. She always reminds me of the time—and they tell this story over and over like a legend—I was two and climbed up on a windowsill. I dangled from the edge, four stories off the ground, just looking down with no worries, but she of course was terrified that I would fall or startle if she called out to me. She says she inched closer and closer and then grabbed me. I was so surprised I started screaming."

"I bet you were a complete rascal."

"Well, she was so easy to taunt because she was so fearful. But it drove me crazy. I was at a swimming pool one summer—maybe I was twelve or eleven—and I didn't want to go home just yet. All of a sudden, her voice came over the loudspeaker ordering, "Ernst Feidler, get out of the pool immediately and come home." Every one went completely silent from the shock and then they laughed their heads off. I dove underwater and stayed down until my lungs burned. I was so humiliated and furious with her for embarrassing me.

"What happened when you got home? Did she spank you?"

"No, that would have been simpler. Instead she cried, 'My heart, my son, you are going to kill me with worry.' And she grabbed her chest and sobbed until I felt so bad I begged for her forgiveness." He paused. "My father was gone a lot so it was just my mother and I most of the time."

"Where was your father?"

"He worked for a textile business and went to the factories in England. He could speak three languages, including Russian." Ernst scoffed, "And he blames me for getting us in trouble because I could speak Russian and English. He taught me!"

"Why did he learn Russian? I can't imagine he had factories there after the revolution."

"No, he fought on the German front. He just had a knack for language, like I do. Sometimes it's a curse." Ernst threw his hand over his face and then he sat on the side of the bed. "He was talented but what a waste. A textile factory manager. Well, not me."

"Of course not. We're going back to California."

He looked at her abruptly, his expression dark, veiled. "I am grateful that Mutti forced me to learn the violin. Otherwise I'd just be another nationalist cog in the wheel." He shook his head and sat up. "Let's go back downstairs. I have to take a blood test before surgery."

The next day Ernst went into surgery. He came through the operation without complications. Their afternoons in the attic were lovely and fruitful. Their love and commitment was rekindled, and by the time Ernst had to go back to active duty in the United States, Manou was pregnant again.

Manou returned to La Bâtie for the rest of the summer, where the women of her family doted on her for the first time in her life. She loved sitting back with her fat baby on her lap, watching the family hustle about. Karl looked around with big, dark eyes, calmly taking it all in.

In August, Manou went to Lyon to get her visa. She had the problem of different last names for herself and Karl, and no US marriage license to validate her reason for permission to return legally. Knowing there was no lie that could explain the oddity of her documents, she opted to tell the consulate the truth. With a little embellishment and flirtation—because it worked when she wanted to go to Iowa—she convinced the consulate to issue her a visa. "Your story is sweet. I admire your commitment," he said with a shy smile as he handed her a temporary visa. "When you actually get married," he added, "you can apply for permanent resident status like Ernst's." In October, Manou and Karl flew into New York. Ernst was stationed at Fort Belvoir, Virginia, for classes, so he took a train to the city to meet her. She was glad to see the surgery had brought him back to his full robust self. When they got back to the base, they went to a justice of the peace in Alexandria to get married. Manou's new dress draped over her pregnant abdomen while she held baby Karl in her arms, but no one blinked an eye.

Ernst finished his classes and was reassigned to the Army Language Institute in Pacific Grove. He bought an old Chevy sedan and the two lovers, now a family of almost four, drove back across the country over many of the same roads of their life-altering journey west a year and a half earlier. Manou couldn't put words to the aura of promise and the sense of liberation that saturated every cell of her body. She just held Karl tight and grinned as Ernst whistled snippets of Mozart, Brahms, and Bach.

♫

In the lonely summer evenings fifteen years later, when the kids slept and Maman read quietly in the guest room, Manou went through the boxes of her letters to Ernst. She had written 200 of them from the fall of 1953 to spring 1954, one almost every day, and he had kept them all. His letters were much shorter than hers, and less frequent but they had moved her deeply. Once he wrote, *Don't let anything or anyone bother you in France, my love. You have me.* The driving force of their union was to evolve a wholly new organism from the conjoined seeds of their traditions. Redefining themselves and their family in California was a mutual crusade.

Manou looked through a photo album from Ernst's childhood. She knew what she had flown from—and towards—but she had never been entirely sure why he took wing with an even greater fervor than hers. All the façade of German perfection surrounded him. There was a picture of him as a cherubic two-year-old walking in a pine forest, Mutti smiling behind him. There was the handsome blond youth dressed in lederhosen, hiking boots, and a cap, sitting under the bucolic Bavarian Alps. There was a stiff, self-important adolescent Ernst in a pinstriped suit, and another picture of him trying out for a Mr. Universe contest, sticking out his flexed chest with somber pride.

What were the thoughts behind these poses? Manou wondered. What shaped Ernst into such a confusing closed man? All the things I don't know. All the questions I never asked, she berated herself. Now she never could. Why did he never speak of the war and the Russian occupation? What were his activities that drove the family from East Germany, as Mutti had insinuated? Why did he get this guilty, profoundly sad look when they talked about his homeland? Why did he always say with a wry smile that he would not live past forty? Why had Manou thought he was joking?

Giga

The Folk Dance

Manou and the children learned not to talk about Ernst, although he was a shadowy presence behind them every day. With four children and work, Manou resorted to the style that had shaped their marriage: throwing herself into action as they had thrown themselves into life as a young couple in Pacific Grove. She resolved to move forward, to control her family environment regardless of what was compromising, realigning, or crumbling inside her.

In August, after Maman left, Ernst's department chairman from Valley College called her.

"Hello, Mrs. Feidler?"

"Yes, that's me."

"This is Charlie Reston, from the college."

Manou's stomach clenched as it did every time someone or something emerged from Ernst's life and tapped on the round hollow drum of her grief. She had talked to Maman about possibly returning to France just to avoid moments like this. Maman had looked briefly hopeful but she knew her daughter. She sighed and said, "You've been in California for fifteen years. This is your home and your children's home. Besides, you can't make that kind of change when you are still in shock. Tell yourself to carry on. Yes, you can carry on."

Charlie cleared his throat and Manou realized he was waiting for a response. "Oh yes, Charlie. We met once didn't we? At a department picnic?"

"Yes. Last summer. I'm calling because we're in a jam and I was hoping you might be able to help us out."

"I'm not sure how I can help but tell me what you need."

"Well," Charlie coughed a little, either out of nervousness or the Winston cigarettes he chain-smoked.

Manou remembered that at the picnic he had lit one cigarette after another and she had to move Francis away from him because his eyes had teared from the smoke. She wasn't against an occasional cigarette but American men seemed to consume them like candy. "Well, since your husband died ... I mean, since he passed away so suddenly, we are short an instructor in the language department. He mentioned that you teach, too, and I was wondering if you'd be available to work at Valley this fall."

She had earned her master's in French during the whirlwind years, part of keeping pace with her ever-galloping husband.

"I know you teach high school French. We have someone who can teach German and Russian but that leaves the French classes without an instructor."

Manou considered his offer. "But I am under contract to Contra Costa High School."

Charlie laughed. "I know your principal Jerry Thomson pretty well. I think we could make an arrangement. We would have a full schedule for you and the pay is better."

Manou had been worried about the dwindling life insurance and the near-empty bank account without two incomes, but it was the prospect of teaching older students and working in a college environment that suddenly began to excite her. She agreed to go to Valley and meet with Charlie.

After going over her class list at Valley, Manou understood that college time schedules did not conform to her children's public school schedules. It was going to be difficult to juggle their lives and hers. She needed help. Maman couldn't do it because she had had enough of America after the short month of her summer visit. Marraine was not well and her sister Odette had her own family to take care of. Mutti was the only one who was available. She had come to stay for many extended visits, especially when the family grew by one member every eleven months for four years.

Yet, the visits with Mutti had been mixed blessings. It certainly gave both Ernst and Manou much freedom to pursue their diverse interests. She took care of everything in her meticulous way but her fawning over Ernst always made Manou feel inadequate as a wife. Questioning everything about her marriage now, Manou wondered if Mutti's availability created a chasm more than a bond between two fulfilled yet disconnected adults? Nonetheless, Manou's obligation to provide for the family left her no choice but to call Hof, Germany, and ask her mother-in-law to take care of domestic minutia once again while Manou taught. Also, Manou felt the desire to reach out to Mutti because Max had died. Perhaps the two widows could offer some comfort and solace to each other.

Three weeks later Manou drove to the airport with hope but also with trepidation about the emotional landmines the dour Mutti could detonate at the most unexpected, often most vulnerable, moments.

♫

Unlike the grimy neighborhoods of South Los Angeles, Pacific Grove on the Monterrey Peninsula at first seemed like a mecca for PFC Ernst Feidler and his family. In 1954, after basic training, he was promoted and recruited to teach in the Army Language Institute on the base. Manou took care of a drafty old wood house where Karl's marbles rolled from the center of the room to the wall without being pushed. From the front yard, they only had to walk two blocks to cross onto dunes above the beach. How could anyone feel poor in such a place? Manou had thought when she first moved there. She walked to the beach daily, balancing Karl and a picnic basket on either side of her enormous belly. She almost felt giddy, next to the sea, amid asters, primroses, sand verbena, and tufts of silvery hair-grass. The Pacific was an idyllic deep blue, the hillsides were covered with pines, and the misty fog burned into a soft light every noon.

When their second child, Sophia, was born, Manou did not receive the solicitous postpartum attention of the French medical system. She was home in two short days and abruptly discovered her maternal disposition had its limits. Where was Marraine? Where was Grand-mère? There was no extended family of women to carry on with domestic chores and no washing machine to take care of the diapers and clothes for two—then in another eleven months, three—children all under four. Manou was overwhelmed. She had to sterilize bottles in a canning kettle on the stove and cook her own baby food because they couldn't afford jars of Gerber carrots and Motts applesauce.

As much as she basked in the gorgeous coast, her California life became the opposite of what she had romantically imagined in the attic of the Army Hospital in Frankfurt. She'd been nursing or pregnant for three years. Days were routine, without adventure. Mornings were spent bathing, feeding, preparing bottles, and watching over the babies. In the afternoon, she walked them to the beach, lay on the sand in a stupor while they played, and then shopped for dinner on the way home. Back in the little house, it was more baths, feeding, and bedtime, life's events on a predictable and lackluster loop. By afternoon, Manou thought she would drown if she had to change one more diaper or solve one more quarrel over toys. She felt like she disappeared in the endless mind-numbing months of child rearing. She ached for interesting conversation but other mothers only talked about the minutia of living with children. Ernst was too tired to talk because he worked stimulating days at the Army Language Institute where he had been hired as a civilian instructor after he completed his military obligations. He also got angry when she complained.

Yet, after being cooped up in the house all day one Friday when the older two kids were sick with colds, and baby Francis was whining from colic, Manou resolved to ask him for help. When Ernst returned from class, and the kids were as clean and quiet as possible, she cautiously asked, "Could you put them to bed tonight. I've been with them all...."

"I'm tired, Manou. I've had classes all day; can't you do it? You've just been hanging around the house."

"But three kids, two of them sick, is as much work as..."

He slapped his hand on the table making the dishes clatter. "Stop your complaining. I hate that."

Manou looked down at her hands. "I know I shouldn't complain..."

"Then don't."

She couldn't hold back. Her irritation frothed to the surface. "But I'm an educated person, too. I don't want to baby-sit all day every day."

Ernst left the table and slumped in their worn old armchair. "You should have thought of that before you had so many kids, Marie Madeleine." When they argued he spat out her full name as if she were the biblical seductress in person. She knew what would come next: the vilification of her sexuality, an accounting of her lover before she met him, her lust.

"Oh, right, I had them all by myself. You were just asleep when I conceived immaculately. All three times."

"Enough." Ernst ordered. "You're the one who...

Manou walked away before he could devolve into the standard litany of her failures. In the kitchen, she fell into a silent fury that had tormented her since her parents first faulted her for her spirit. In her family, the women condemned and the men punished. She'd often been heartily spanked for breaking things or hiding or simply doing something the wrong way. The men's authority was so deeply ingrained that she didn't challenge Ernst when he took that tone. But she fumed inside. Would she never escape the bad girl image that defined her as a child because she was boyishly rambunctious, and defined her as a woman because she was too erotic? She felt ensnared in a vicious circle of guilt and fear and rebellion as she clattered dinner dishes in the sink.

Karl sniffled and flicked his marbles around the floor. Sophia curled up in her father's lap and he absently stroked her hair while he read. Francis was too little to notice the quarrel. One by one, Manou picked them up and tucked them into bed. She rubbed camphor on Karl and Sophia's chests and sang them a French lullaby. Soon they slept, breathing in and out with little gurgles.

While on the outside she was Mommy, inside she resolved not to be bullied. She had to make Ernst see that the Manou he fell in love with—active and smart and good-humored and, yes, sexual—was slowly drowning. When she returned to the living room, ready to try again, this time with a sweeter tone, Ernst was rubbing his temples as if he had a headache. Ignoring their argument, Ernst dropped his hands and stated, "The school has frozen our salaries."

Manou knew instantly what this meant: who put the kids to bed was the least of their problems. They were already holding off their creditors and had been counting on Ernst's pay raise to cover the bills. "You know I'd gladly get a job, too, but it's not possible with the kids."

"I know, but we quite simply need more money. I found out I could teach extra night classes three times a week in the Pacific Grove Adult Education Program," he paused, "but that means my days will be even longer."

Manou closed her eyes to digest the vision of more time at home with the children, not less. Yet she understood difficult times. The war years in France had taught her well that you don't complain in adversity. You rise to the occasion. Their financial crisis instantly infused her maternal boredom with purpose. "Thank you, Maman," she whispered.

Ernst looked at her curiously. "What did you say?"

"I said, don't worry. I know how to *regarder les choses en face*, to face this, and make do on very little."

His face softened and he reached out his arms. "Come here, Manou." She stood by his chair and he pulled her onto his lap. "Let's all go to Carmel Beach tomorrow. I can do more with the kids on the weekends to help you catch up with things."

The next day seemed like the most beautiful day of their family life to Manou. As she nursed Francis, Ernst carried Karl and Sophia on his shoulders across the sand and dunked them playfully in tidal pools. They examined the many varieties of seaweed: the type with bubbles that popped, the slimy leafy strands, and the one that looked like long strings of rope. After lunch, Karl disappeared into the rocks and Manou panicked when he wasn't back before the tide started rolling in. The whole family went looking for him, calling him in panic until he popped from behind a dune, happy as a lark. Ernst and Manou almost got mad but they exchanged a glance that said the day was too lovely to be ruined. On the drive back to Pacific Grove, Manou looked at her children lying in the backseat, languid from sun and sea air, and she wanted nothing more than to be the best wife and mother she could be. This made her happy.

For the rest of the year, she made it her mission to make do on their miniscule budget. She took the kids to the town of Seaside produce stands for the fruits and vegetables too bruised or wilted for merchants to sell. She turned them into soups, gratins, purees, baby food, and fruit compotes. On Fisherman's Wharf, she got halibut heads and whitefish tails to make delicious soupe de poissons with stale bread croutons. Manou picked wild spinach along the coastal streams and found mushrooms in the pine forests above Pacific Grove. She got cheap tongue and kidneys from a local market and served her stews with homemade baguettes. To the horror of her next-door neighbor, Manou even harvested the miserable little snails that crawled through her yard. Ernst knew how to make beer although more than a few bottles simply blew up in the hot backyard shed. Life was difficult but creative.

It became second nature for Manou to handle the domestic demands during their financial distress, yet she was still insufficiently challenged by homemaking. She was determined to find a way to have a more interesting life. First, she kept herself in good shape with exercises learned in her physical education studies. Under the curious eyes of other women in the neighborhood, she went through her fitness routine every afternoon in the backyard and then showed her kids how to turn cartwheels and somersaults across the lawn. Betty, the same neighbor who was disgusted by the thought of eating snails, hung lethargically on the picket fence between their yards and asked, "Where did you learn all that?"

Manou sat on the grass catching her breath. "I studied physical education in college, Betty."

Betty wistfully murmured, "I wish there was somewhere I could learn how to do that. I'm probably too old."

"Don't be silly. You're younger than I am and anyone can learn fitness at any age," Manou declared. This planted a seed, as if she had experienced an epiphany. Always appalled by the lack of physical activity of the women around her, Manou vowed to show them how good it felt. Why not start some classes for women? Only Jack La Lanne and Bonnie Pruden were remote TV images of physical fitness.

Before mentioning anything to Ernst, she called the Pacific Grove Adult Education Program and proposed her idea: a two-night per week fitness class for women—Tuesday and Thursday, when Ernst didn't teach. They reluctantly agreed to try a four-week pilot program, and Ernst halfheartedly approved of it because it would help pay the bills.

With the kids in tow, Manou passed mimeographed flyers around the neighborhood. Only two students showed up for the first class, but by the fourth, word had reached the languishing women of Pacific Grove.

They flocked to the old high school gymnasium to run, stretch, jump, and do abdominal exercises with the charming, attractive French physical education teacher. Just like in her days at the University of Iowa, the local press showed up and photographed Manou in all kinds of positions including standing on her head. *Manou Feidler*, the reporter wrote, *was an exotic anomaly in the world of American womanhood: an athlete.* Manou felt like a pioneer and her students told her they felt like "a million bucks." She also opened a Wednesday morning dance class for children, partly so she could bring her own kids to the gym.

One important transition metamorphosed into another. A physical fitness student asked Manou if she would tutor her in French for an upcoming trip to Paris. Manou put on her only decent dress, a red one Maman had sent her, left her current modest circumstances, and for a few hours stepped into her student's fairy tale world of ease across the peninsula in Pebble Beach. They sipped tea and savored petites fours in a stunning parlor overlooking the Pacific, and discussed a current article in *Paris Match* or a classic French novel by Victor Hugo or Alexandre Dumas.

When she returned to her den, Manou wondered aloud to Ernst, "Do these people have any worries?"

"They have worries. Just not the same as ours."

Manou looked around their messy house and sighed. "Couldn't you pick up just a little? Sometimes?"

Ernst frowned. "I played with the kids the whole time. What more do you want?"

Manou began to toss toys in the toy chest. "I know, I know. You are far too busy but I'm not."

Karl tugged at her sleeve. "Mama, can we have some supper?"

She scowled back at Ernst. "And I suppose you can't feed them either!"

Already lost behind a book, he ignored her sarcasm.

As she fed and bathed the three little Feidlers, she heard Ernst practicing his violin downstairs. She paused as she was towel-drying Sophia. It was the first time he had played in a long time. Francis tapped his ducky on the bathwater to the timing of his scales. Manou squatted back on her haunches next to the tub and smiled. No matter how disgruntled she was, his music reached inside her and moved her, imperceptibly, like a changing tide.

When she went back downstairs, he was just putting his instrument back in the case. The dishes were still in the sink but she was done being angry. "It's good to hear the music again," she said wistfully. "I love when you play."

"Manou, I have an idea." She scrapped the plates into the garbage and ran hot water into the sink. He stood next to her and turned the water off. "Did you hear me? I have an idea."

"You always have ideas...in five languages." She turned the water back on. "but can we talk about it over breakfast? I'm pretty tired."

He turned the water back off. "My idea is a solution for you, too. Sit down and listen."

"Fine." Manou sat at the table and folded her arms.

"Why don't we ask Mutti to come help us for a few months? That way you can have time for your classes and the house chores will be taken care of."

The image of the stern German woman popped into Manou's head and she did not relish her grim disposition in their lives on a daily basis. Then she looked around the kitchen at the piles of dishes, overflowing laundry basket, and grimy floors, and like a split frame, she simultaneously imagined Mutti's tidy little apartment, everything in its place.

"But we don't have a room for her."

"We can fix up the room over the garage."

"What about your father?"

"He's used to being alone. Besides, she'd only stay for a few months, just enough time to help us get things under control."

"Let me think a minute, Ernst." So many carrots dangled in front of Manou's nose: time to teach, a clean house, a grandmother nanny.

"And one other thing."

"Yes?"

"I found out I can use the GI Bill to get a degree in music from San Jose State."

She nodded. Now she understood his real motive. He had become as stuck in his rut of teaching foreign languages and being tied down to the family as she was. He was never more fulfilled than when he played his violin, and she loved him more when he was happy. The resonance of music in the house would be a bonus. "Yes," Manou agreed. "Let's invite Mutti to stay for awhile. But I have one condition."

"What's that?"

"I will do the cooking."

Ernst grinned. "Understood."

Ernst led her upstairs and they made love, having crossed the chasm of another argument, recovering their illusive balance without asking—or answering—too many questions.

Before Mutti arrived a month later, again Manou sat down with Ernst after the kids were in bed, this time with different news. She put her head on her hands at the kitchen table and muttered, "I'm pregnant again. About eight weeks."

Neither of them smiled. "Well," Ernst finally said, "we always said we wanted a big family."

Manou let out a long breath. "Four kids," she said gazing at his handsome face, a little tired but completely alert to the consequences of her words. She touched his cheek lightly. "Our children are always beautiful, aren't they?"

"And smart, too. I'm already teaching Karl some Russian words."

"Sophia sang one of my French lullabies yesterday. All of it with perfect pitch. I almost cried."

They sat quietly. Ernst finally added with a shrug. "You can teach for about four more months."

"Five. I'll start again when the baby is three months old."

"Mutti is coming."

"I'm glad," Manou admitted.

Manou and the kids picked up Mutti at the San Francisco airport because Ernst had already started classes for his music degree. Mutti got off the plane wearing a dark wool skirt and pressed white blouse buttoned up to her chin. Manou marveled at how she had remained so neat after sixteen hours of travel, yet her mother-in-law looked out of place next to the casual Californians milling around the baggage claim. But Sophia and Karl hugged their grandmother's legs and welcomed her with their bubbling affection. When Mutti entered the drafty little house, she shrugged and stated, "I will begin." She unpacked her apron and sensible brown shoes, and then went to the kitchen and started wiping the windows over the sink, but too tired from her long trip, she retired early.

The next day, Ernst walked in the door at six for dinner. Dancing around Mutti cleaning the cupboards and scrubbing the linoleum floor, Manou had managed to cook a pork cassoulet. They had a robust family dinner with Mutti constantly popping up to serve and clear and wipe up the children's spills. Manou almost laughed because her mother-in-law resembled a dervish jack-in-the-box, but it was tiring by the end of the meal and she wished the woman would relax. Surely Mutti was just trying to prove her worth and would settle into a more tempered routine.

After dinner, Manou went to tutor her Pebble Beach student. When she walked in the back door two hours later, the kitchen was immaculate, the toys put away, and there was no sound of children. She put her coat in the hall closet and called out, "Ernst? Mutti?" Puzzled by the stillness in her normally energetic household, she entered the living room and stopped in her tracks.

Ernst was resting in an armchair with his eyes closed. Mutti was on her hands and knees on the floor in front of him with a pan of water. Ernst's bare feet were in the pan and his mother was washing them with a cloth. His mother wiped each toe as she picked his feet up, placed them on a towel, and rubbed them dry. Manou felt a wave of embarrassment for the woman's servile behavior, then disgust. Manou would never behave like that towards any child and certainly not towards a grown man. But when Ernst opened his eyes and saw her in the doorway, he merely asked, "How was your tutorial?" as if having his mother wash his feet was the most normal thing in the world.

Mutti turned to her and her face lit up with a rare smile. "Ernst had a fine practice session. He is working on a sonata and it is coming along, isn't it, *meine Liebe?*"

"It is, Mutti."

"But the children were quite disruptive. I had to tell them many times to sit quietly, especially Karl. Manou," she scolded, "you must be firmer with him." She sighed and returned to drying her son's feet.

Day in and day out, the pattern was the same: Manou and Ernst came and left as their work schedules demanded and Mutti maintained the home front. The children adapted to their grandmother's gruff style. Although Sophia occasionally complained about Mutti's scolding or Karl said he had been spanked with the wooden spoon, they were generally happy, especially Francis who was Mutti's favorite. She stroked his little blond head and said, "*Ach mein liebes Kleines.*" On Saturdays, Ernst took the kids off for an outing and on Sunday Mutti rested in her little room over the garage. Ernst joined the local Music Chamber, practiced for hours, and performed somewhere in the area every week.

Sometimes the cacophony of Ernst's scales, children's quibbling, and Mutti's reprimands was grating, but Manou said nothing, restraining herself, thinking her mood was the normal irritability of pregnancy. Her husband, after all, was in high spirits. Her mother-in-law took care of the chores she hated. The children were healthy and normal.

One Sunday Ernst returned from his recital calling out, "Hey, everybody!" When Manou came to the top of the stairs and looked down at him, she saw that flushed face and impish grin she knew so well. It signaled an imminent declaration of a notion in his head and a fire in his belly that would move their lives heartily in one direction or another.

Mutti was resting in her room but she had heard her son's exuberant tone of voice and appeared at the top of the stairs, too. "What's happening?"

He spread his arms as if embracing the world. "We are going to build a house."

Manou trotted downstairs saying, "A house! You are crazy. We don't even have one cent. And you have to know how to build. How in the world..."

"I do know how to build. I helped put up a barn in North Dakota the summer before you came to Iowa." He brought his hands together palms up. "Building is really easy. In this country, you can do it yourself as long as you follow code. Look, I was talking to Phillip Bennett..."

"You mean the realtor in your Chamber group?"

"Yes. That guy. You met him at the concert at the Episcopalian church a few weeks ago. Anyway, I was bemoaning the fact that I've got a fourth kid coming and I'll never be able to save enough money for a down payment on a home. He said I could get a lot for a fraction of the money and build as the cash comes in." Mutti had descended the stairs, too, and was listening intently. "Come in the kitchen, both of you. I'm dying of thirst but I've got to tell you the rest of this." He filled a tall glass at the sink and drank it down, gulping like a kid. He put the glass in the sink and pointed at Manou. "You'll see. One year from now, we'll be rich. And you are going to help me."

"But," Manou began, yet she paused as she saw the resolute set of his brow, his eyes shining with confidence, the way his body towered in its full height, and his sarcastic little smile that seemed to say, "I know you don't believe me." She understood that trying to stop this scheme would be like throwing herself in front of a rushing locomotive. And his faith was compelling. Why not follow the enterprising giant in front of her?

Like a dancer who obscures a missed step with an entirely new move, she revised her tone. "Okay, let me just ask a couple of questions."

"Fair enough."

"Where do we get the money?"

"Bennett knows of some acre parcels that only need a fifty dollar down payment."

"Why so cheap?"

"It's a little hilly, I guess."

She paused. Bad land? It seemed like Ernst wasn't thinking it through, which was unlike him.

"But," he added as if revealing a tantalizing secret, "it is zoned R-2. For duplexes."

Both women stared at him, digesting the whole scene now. "Ah," said Mutti. "build two and then live in one and..."

"Rent the other. Exactly." Ernst's eyes burst from his face, like he had finally found a treasure map.

"Okay, I get the financial angle, too. We can probably come up with fifty dollars," Manou said, "but I know nothing about building a house and I can just see myself teetering on a scaffold, eight months pregnant, in case you've forgotten." She also imagined pipes bursting, floors crumbling, and the roof collapsing in a kind of domino effect of bad construction.

"Manou, you can do this. It's basic," he said, his smile exuding such bone-crushing strength, such confidence in what was beyond the possible that she was already sold in her core. Nonetheless, she waited for him to justify it to her still doubting edges. "We draw up very straightforward plans. The house's skeleton is fit together with precut joists, studs, beams, and rafters. The windows and doors fit into the skeleton like Karl's building blocks. The siding is nailed on the outside and sheetrock panels cover the inside like skins. You know the rest." He gave her that unassailable smile again. "Remember Jack and Edith's? Plaster, paint, floors, tiles, cabinets. We restored that place in a few weeks."

"How do we keep from electrocuting ourselves?"

Ernst waved away her concerns. "Obviously we hire out the jobs we can't do ourselves like electrical and plumbing. We just need a tape measure, a power saw, hammers, and a level." He turned to his mother. "But we can't do it without you, Mutti, especially with the baby coming. I know you only planned to stay a few months but..."

Mutti nodded. "I'll call Max," she said as she walked toward the living room. "How long?" she called over her shoulder.

"Tell him you'll be home soon."

After they purchased the property, Ernst and Manou went to the site every night after work and every weekend. Mutti took care of the children and occasionally brought them to the site, but she was focused on the responsibilities of her domestic domain. This included doting on Ernst when he came home, because he must be "so tired from such a long day," washing his feet and massaging his shoulders. Manou ignored this interaction, too tired to muster annoyance with her mother-in-law, and went straight to the tub where she rested her growing womb and weary back in bath salts. She'd moan with relief yet often wondered what had happened to their life as a couple.

After they cleared the site together, the Feidler construction team of two each had designated tasks, but Manou found herself handling many details alone because they needed to be done during the work day. Ernst left her in charge of many important tasks. For instance, when the concrete mixer was scheduled to pour the foundation one morning at 9 a.m., the building inspector came and said the corners of the forms weren't fortified well enough. Yet the truck was due to arrive in an hour and Ernst had told her the inspection was a mere formality. It turned out that the man refused to approve the forms. Manou fell into an internal panic, thinking Ernst would ridicule her if she let herself be bullied out of the costly cement. So she used her most reliable tool: her feminine wiles. She rubbed her protruding belly and sighed in distress. "But my husband said it would be so simple. What can I do? We can't afford to pay for the unused cement." She bent down and picked up a reinforcing rod. "I guess I can put these in myself," and she tapped at it weakly near the form.

The inspector took off his cap and scratched his head. "Don't do that, missus. You might hurt yourself." He went around the periphery of the house adding rods as needed. She coyly cradled a handful of the two-foot precut steel bars and followed him around the periphery of the foundation, demurely offering him one every time he said, "Here," or "This corner will fall out, too," or "Another." They finished the last one just as the concrete mixer rounded the bend and squealed to a stop at the construction site. Ouf! She was saved.

The duplex rose from the hillside, and just as Manou had imagined, one day she stood alone on a scaffold painting clapboard siding, layer upon layer, with her belly protruding between a paint bucket and the view of Monterey Bay in front of her. That same day she felt the first contractions of labor, and she drove herself to the hospital instead of her fitness class. The labor to bring little Florence into the Feidler family seemed neat and swift compared to the sustained effort of building the duplex, and Manou welcomed the few days of rest to nurse and meet her fourth child. Mutti was unusually solicitous, and Manou received gentle nurturing from her three youngsters.

Within six months, Ernst and Manou stood on the front porch of the duplex with a glass of wine to celebrate the notice of completion. Manou watched the setting sun reflect orange and red off the flawless plate glass windows overlooking the bay. *We did it!* she thought, feeling very proud. Manou was ready to dance and sing about their achievement and to praise Ernst for his good judgment. They already had a prospective tenant for Unit B at a monthly rent that almost paid off the loan. She turned to Ernst to tell him how she had doubted, how he had been right, and how much she loved him. But his expression was odd. He gazed over the building and the landscape with a slight frown. His eyes looked dull, unenthusiastic, as if the show were over and it hadn't been that good. As if none of it measured up to some unspoken expectation. She touched his arm but he shook off her hand and went into the house to answer the new phone.

Manou saw what was happening, and she was saddened by his disappointment, by his unwillingness to celebrate. She watched him through the window. He was standing in the freshly painted empty room listening, and then he stiffened, scowled, and said something into the receiver, perhaps asked a question. He hung up and stood there a moment, framed all around by depthless white. He seemed suspended, expressionless and motionless. Then he cocked his head like a dog listening to something high pitched. He shook it off, looked out the window, and saw Manou watching. Ernst walked out to the porch. "We have to go back to the other house."

"What is it. You look so..."

"It's Max. He's sick. Mutti must go back to Germany."

Only later did Manou recall that he had said "Max," not my father or papa, that he was cool and controlled as if talking about someone unrelated.

"Come with me," Mutti begged her son the night before she left, grabbing his shoulders with uncharacteristic insistence.

He put her hands down at her sides. "You know I can't. I have to work."

"But your father is so sick."

Ernst turned away for a minute then looked back at his mother and smiled. "We'll come soon. The whole family. We'll visit all the relatives. Right, Manou?"

Take the little ones to Europe? What a handful, she thought. "I suppose we could do that," she said uncertainly.

"Promise?" insisted Mutti.

"I promise."

Without her mother-in-law, Manou resumed taking care of the children all day and offering fitness classes and tutorials in the evening. That winter Ernst finished his degree in music, but instead of teaching music, in the spring he accepted a better job teaching languages at the Valley College up in the Bay area. The job would begin in the fall so he devised a big family summer road trip. "Let's vacation before I start the new job. We can sell the duplex and use the money to go to Europe." His plan was to load everyone in a VW bus, chug across the U.S to New York where they would catch a ship to Le Havre. In June, they sold everything they owned, except the violin and a few mementos, which they put in storage, and took off across the country with the kids. They camped with army surplus gear and held an 8-millimeter camera out the window of the van to film wildlife at Yellowstone, American presidents at Mount Rushmore, and every other landmark they passed to show their families abroad. During a stopover with friends in Illinois, Ernst made a call to Mutti in Hof. She told him that his father had taken a turn for the worse. Max was dying, and Ernst needed to get there as fast as possible.

"I have to fly out of Chicago in the morning. You bring the kids as planned and I'll meet you there," he told Manou.

"Oh no! I'm sorry about your father but...how am I going to do that?" she asked him frantically that night in the bedroom. Camping with four kids under the age of six had been challenging enough with two adults but making the rest of the way to Europe alone with them seemed totally insurmountable.

He waved his hand in irritation. "You'll manage. We already have tickets on the S.S. Ascania. Just get to New York. Okay?" He rolled away from her on the bed and refused to talk about it anymore.

They dropped him off at the airport the next morning where he disappeared into a throng of travelers. Manou sat idling the VW at the terminal, afraid and powerless. She turned off the engine and told the kids to sit quietly while she thought about what to do. She got out of the car and walked up and down in front of the departing travelers, angry that he had insisted on another event—almost as huge as building the duplex—and then left her picking up the pieces when he couldn't follow through. "But, Manou," she scolded herself. "His father is dying. It is not his fault..."

"*He could have helped you figure out how to get to New York,*" her other voice interrupted.

"He is grieving."

"*He has known this could happen since Mutti left last fall. He could have planned more sensibly.*"

"Since when is Ernst sensible?"

"*Never about emotional things. He counts on you for that.*"

"Well then. I have to handle this, don't I?" The question became a statement of purpose. "I will handle this."

After twenty minutes, she had her plan.

First, she did not want to drive across Illinois, Indiana, and Ohio to New York with four little kids. She had to be able to feed the baby and keep the others out of trouble. Manou drove to the train station in downtown Chicago to get tickets to New York. Then she drove to a used car lot and sold the VW complete with the army surplus blankets, cots, cook-stove, and tent. They caught a bus back downtown and arrived just in time to get on the cross-country train to Grand Central Station in Manhattan.

It was a forty-eight-hour trip that felt like a month. She juggled the four of them as they crawled all over the seats, ran up the aisles, and demanded food and drink and toys every few minutes night and day. During one brief hiatus when all four were sprawled asleep across the seats, Manou couldn't rest for worrying about where to stay and how to get around in New York City. "It won't be as bad as my first arrival," she reassured herself. "At least I am now a citizen and I speak English."

Two days later, she poured off the train lugging two giant suitcases along with the flock of children. A taxi took them to a "reasonably priced" hotel but when they got to the twenty-fifth floor and parked their stuff in the tiny room with two double beds and one window, she realized it had no air-conditioning and the city was in a mid-summer heat wave. She undressed all four musky-smelling children and sat them in a tepid bath, the toddler propped between Karl's knees. "Just one night," she muttered. "Then we'll be on the ship with a nursery." She called the Italian shipping line to confirm their reservation.

"Sorry. There's been a delay. The longshoremen are on strike and you'll have to call back in three days."

"*Merde!*" she yelled.

"Beg pardon, Ma'am?"

"Nothing. I'll call back." And she collapsed on the bed pounding a pillow.

What was she going to do with her darling jumping beans for half a week in the city? The first morning she took them out for breakfast, but it was nearly impossible to keep them together through the rush-hour crowds on the street. Manou ducked into a hardware store and bought two leashes to hook onto two-year-old Florence and Francis while Karl and Sophia held their hands. She also bought four identical red children's coveralls so if they did escape she'd spot them right away. They looked like a team of dogs walking down the streets of Manhattan.

After donuts and milk, they spent the first day in the air-conditioned Museum of Natural History, leaving only to get hot dogs and ice cream for lunch. In the evening after the tired little bodies draped across the two beds, Manou washed the coveralls in the tub and hung them by the grimy window to dry overnight. They spent the next day at the Central Park Zoo, wandering past every cage, pausing as long as possible in the cool reptile house, and again eating hotdogs and ice cream for meals.

The following day her goal was to walk them to every little park within a reasonable distance of their hotel so the kids could play on the swings or roll in the grass. Karl acted like the responsible big brother until he got tired, then he collapsed on a bench and refused to move. Sophia was thrilled with the store display windows and wanted to stop at every one. Florence and Francis were toddlers who alternated between giggles and whining.

That night, Manou called to find out about the S.S. Ascania's departure, she was informed that the strike was not over so the ship was going to depart from Montreal instead of New York. The company would pay for their train fare to catch the boat in Canada in twenty-four hours. "*Merde!*" Manou shouted again after she hung up. But after some more satisfying pillow punching, in the morning she packed up the two suitcases, leashed up the kids, each now with their plastic dinosaur from the museum, hailed a cab, and trudged through Grand Central to catch the train to Montreal.

After reining in the monkeys on the seats and fetching their dinosaurs from the aisles for several more hours, she caught a bus from the central train station to the St. Lawrence River dock in Montreal. It was crowded with hundreds of passengers that had been displaced by the strike. They were all tired and irritated but Manou just barreled her troupe through to the gangway. No one wanted to get onto the Ascania and set sail for Le Havre more than a mother who had survived New York in a heat wave with four small children.

After a dinner that was yet another feat of child-controlling gymnastics, Manou asked the steward what time the nursery opened in the morning.

"Oh, Madame," he said looking surprised at her request. "We have no nursery on this ship since most of the passengers are students."

Manou stared at him. In her head she yelled, "*Merde!*" louder than ever, but she calmly ordered, "Let me talk to the captain, please."

The captain soon knocked on her stateroom door in his crisp white uniform. Karl, Sophia, and Francis were jumping on the beds and Florence was howling. Manou calmly stated, "I understand there is no nursery on this ship."

The captain needed no further explanation. He tipped his cap and said, "We will assign a maid to look after the children every day. Enjoy your passage, Madame Feidler."

"*Vous êtes très gentil. Merci.*" Manou then spent the most wonderful crossing of her life. The maid took the children to explore the ship and fed them pastries and pizza right out of the kitchen. The students played shuffleboard and cards with them on deck. Manou ate the most delicious Italian food with great company, she went to movies and parties, and she got to swim in the pool twice a day. They arrived in France on July 13, 1959, exactly one month after the family had departed from Pacific Grove in the VW bus.

Before disembarking, she dressed the kids in cute outfits so Maman wouldn't say, "They look so *américains*." But her parents were absolutely warm and dear at their first sight of their grandchildren. "These children are so adorable!" they exclaimed, and then they drove them straight to La Bâtie where more relatives awaited them: Marraine, Odette, their cousins, and their great grandparents, although Manou's grand-mère terrified the American children instantly by chasing all the children out of the kitchen with a broom.

Over the course of the summer, Manou reacquainted herself with the playful rhythms of La Bâtie. Ernst and Mutti arrived after Max's funeral, which they had insisted was a very small affair and no family needed to come. Ernst arrived tired and withdrawn but seemed to revive at the beautiful house in the mountains as he fished the ice-cold creeks, taught the children how to swim, and when they walked the trails that Manou had walked for more than twenty years, some of his old passion was rekindled under the gorgeous cliffs where he and Manou went to picnic. He would draw her down into the grass next to a brook and make love to her as he hadn't done for months.

The collective of women in the kitchen prepared specialties that Manou had almost forgotten: *lapin chasseur*, *oeufs à la neige*, and fruit pies. Manou sat under the linden tree after lunch, full of exquisite food and a glass of wine, just as she had observed her elders doing every summer. Sophia ran up to her with a spear fashioned from a branch and declared, "We must stay here forever!" and she ran off with her cousins into the woods. "*Garçon manqué*," said Marraine with a wink. Manou stretched out in a lounge chair and muttered, "Ah, Sophia has taken up the torch. But not me anymore. This is so lovely," exhaling a long sweet breath. Marraine and Maman looked at her with open grins, as if to say, "You have joined the secret society of tired mothers!"

Mutti seemed quiet at La Bâtie but not terribly aggrieved. After she arrived, she had resumed her custom of washing not only Ernst's feet but also Manou's father's feet. At first, Papa refused. "No, no. This is too much, Madame Feidler!" but Mutti pushed him gently back into a chair. Papa threw up his hands at every one around him. Soon Mutti had his shoes and socks off and placed Papa's feet in the basin of warm water. His body instantly relaxed and he acquiesced to the strange custom. Mutti had found her niche in the bustle of wives and mothers who took care of the men in one way or another.

Maman looked askance at Manou and led her into the kitchen. "What on earth is Madame Feidler doing? I have never seen such a thing."

Manou, glad for once to have her mother as a cohort, shrugged. "She's always done this for Ernst. It must be a German custom."

"It is certainly not French. You don't have to do this for your husband, do you?"

"Absolutely not, Maman!" And Manou felt a kinship with her mother she had never felt before.

"If it weren't for Ernst's new job, I could actually imagine moving back to France," Manou confided in Marraine the night before they departed for America.

"That would be delightful!" exclaimed her favorite aunt.

"My children would continue speaking French and come to La Bâtie every summer just as I did."

"Perhaps the first part would come true," said Marraine, "but I am going to sell La Bâtie. There is just too much work to be done on the house to maintain it for a few weeks of summer visits. There is the roof, the pipes... I'll have a new, smaller place built instead."

As Marraine went through the litany of problems, Manou felt something fall very far and very fast inside her. La Bâtie symbolized the most profound connection between the members of her family. She had just rediscovered the value of this and now it was done. Over. Never to be experienced again. She wept after everyone had gone to bed and wrote a long poem about La Bâtie in a journal.

The Last Night

This night is the last, in our beloved home
Pépé, you are long gone and you, Mémé.
Marraine, do you hear my pain?
Finality strikes
As tears come to my eyes.
Hope?
Is there?
Is it truly the last night?
I hate hope.
Why keep its flame alive when I know the end is here.

La Bâtie
meadows, forests, the river,
the air so sweet I breathed from the day I was born.
Will I ever walk down the shady lane to the mill again
With all of you, my loves, my strength?
Oh, give me hope... just a little!
A balm in my heart promised that you would never change.
That part of me that cries
Why must it be the last night?
Why?

I will leave, I will love,
Other homes, other shores.
It feels like I'll betray you, for you were the best.
All that being a child incarnates is here,
In La Bâtie.
Am I losing it forever?
I'll seek the happiness that I had known here,
Everywhere.
Will I ever know that feeling again?
Will I retrieve my childhood heart?

There will be other nights
Which will be last nights.
The only one I will not know
Will come some day,
And that night, that one,
will certainly be the last.

By the middle of the night, Manou felt a piece of her self crack off. She had no idea if she would be able to recover it or replicate it ever again in her life. She thought not.

They sailed back to New York on a ship called the Liberté, yet Manou felt nothing of the liberated joy that America had always symbolized for her. Life was punctuated with one responsibility after another. Lulled by the swell from the upper deck, she daydreamed about the calm beauty of La Bâtie, the antithesis of the frenzied life of her big family and her relentless husband ahead. The sea voyage was the last they would take to or from Europe. The age of air travel had dawned and the elegant leisure travel on the ocean liner was over.

Ernst and Manou returned to California just in time to step on the conveyor belt of changes of the 1960s when the Bay Area became a center for new ideas in all the things that propelled the Feidlers' life: parenting, psychology, relationships, music, and art. It made the rest of America seem as Old World as Europe.

♫

Ten years later, Manou sat in front of her bedroom window correcting papers from her classes at Valley College. She noticed that there was suddenly no wind off the bay, and she stopped writing. As the silence enfolded the room, her fist slowly closed up around her pen, her teeth clenched, and her body tensed as if preparing for an enormous effort. Something moved in her body, muffled deep inside her, something that made her afraid. Her fists clenched tighter. She felt like her skin was a dam or a levy holding back a storm surge.

Mutti was in the guest bedroom downstairs, or perhaps scrubbing the floors because she often couldn't sleep. She had come to help but arrived all dressed in black, aged more than the ten years since her husband had died. Manou knew Mutti was grieving for her son, but in a naïve wish, she had hoped she and Mutti could find common ground, a kind of companionship in their mutual loss and confusion. But Mutti's darkness saturated everything.

The day she arrived, Manou and the kids showed her around the Walnut Creek house they had moved into a year ago. Mutti pouted her lips as she gazed in disdain at their large front porch. "It's not the one he built," she said with a sniff of disapproval. "Ernst never liked this place."

"Yes, he did," snapped Karl under his breath.

"Come see, Mutti," said Francis as he pulled her to the backyard. "Look at the pool. We've been swimming all summer."

"Ostentatious," she grumbled and turned away.

Francis was crushed. "But we…"

Manou held his shoulders. "Mutti, it was something Ernst had planned before he died. We thought it was important to finish it…for the kids. In his memory."

"This is not a real memorial."

Manou looked down at Francis and shrugged an apology to him. Manou said, "Come see the rest. You'll be comfortable here.

Mutti followed them in silence into the house. Each room seemed to make Mutti angrier and angrier. Finally, she simply sat in a chair in the living room, clutching her purse. The kids, who were just getting their emotional footing again, couldn't bear the gloom that seeped slowly across the floor like mist in a ghost story, so they backed out of the room. Karl first, then the girls. Francis, always his grandmother's favorite, kissed her cheek, and said, "I'm glad you are here, Mutti." She almost reached out to hug him but caught herself and turned away.

Manou made her a cup of tea, even though Mutti was silent when it was offered. Manou set it in front of her and sat down on the sofa.

Mutti abruptly asked, "What happened to Ernst?"

"I wish I knew. He had the flu but he was also bothered…"

"You didn't watch over him." Mutti fairly spit this accusation across the room. "Not since the first time he came to America and got the thyroid problem."

"Well, he was in the army when that happened. I did take care of him, Mutti, but you know how he refused to accept attention when he was sick."

"He let me care for him. Why not you?"

The blame stung deeply. A thousand thoughts pushed at Manou's fragile levy. She wanted to tell this cold, bitter woman to leave, but her compassion was stronger than her rage, her gratitude for all the help Mutti had given them over the years held her voice. Mutti had been dear then but now she wanted or needed someone to blame for her son's death; that was clear. Manou was the first target. What was a fair defense? It was true that Ernst always let Mutti dote on him. Yet as much as he wanted to be master of the family, he also expected Manou to take charge and materialize his restless visions—like building houses and taking kids across the country—or at least to manage them while he did what he wanted to do. But, Manou knew from experience, Mutti would never accept an imperfect image of the god-like only son. Yet, why did she come here if she was so filled with blame and fury? Mutti was grieving much beyond the grief she had displayed over Max's death that summer at La Bâtie. At that time, she still had her only son. She was now completely alone in the world except for her grandchildren and her daughter-in-law, so Manou decided to be patient.

Manou talked to Mutti briefly about the kids' schedules and what needed to be done to help out. Then she led the despondent woman to her room.

In the morning, Manou drove to Valley College to set up her office. There was a beautiful quad full of students registering for classes in several academic buildings. Charlie Reston led her from Administration to the Foreign Language Department where they walked down the hall to see the language lab and then her French classroom in Room 144, which still had the nametag "Dr. Feidler" in the slot.

"I guess we can leave that," said Reston in front of 144.

"I'm not a PhD," Manou answered.

"Oh, right." He slipped the paper out.

"Just put Marie Madeleine Feidler, please," Manou asked, not sure why she used her formal name.

In the office, the desk was empty but the shelves held as many psychology books as language texts, so she knew they must be Ernst's. As she was setting up her books, posting her calendar and syllabuses on a bulletin board, and putting pictures of the kids on the bookshelf, some of Ernst's colleagues dropped by to welcome her and express their condolences. She recognized a few of them from the funeral and faculty parties. Her stomach clenched all day from the effort of striking the right balance between being the recent widow and the eager new French teacher of Valley College. She just wanted to get into the routine as fast as possible.

Manou arrived at the house in Walnut Creek in time to cook dinner. She expected the usual tidy home and occupied children that Mutti had always provided. Manou walked in the kitchen door to see clothes still piled in the laundry room, dishes in the sink, and kids' footmarks across the floor. Mutti was sitting on the couch in the living room, wearing the same black dress she had arrived in. Francis sat next to her but Sophia and Florence sat stiffly across the room. Mutti was thumbing through one of the family photo albums that Manou had tucked in the back of a cabinet.

"You see, Francis, here you are with your father on the beach at Pacific Grove. Look, do you see how blond his hair got in the sun? Just like yours, Francis."

"*Bonjour, ma famille*," Manou greeted them cheerily. Florence ran to her mother and leaned on her.

"Can I go upstairs now?" asked Sophia.

Without looking at Manou, Mutti said, "You should greet your children in German. So they don't forget."

"Okay, *hallo, meine Familie.* Yes, Sophia, of course you can go upstairs. I'll call you for dinner. Oh, where is Karl?"

"He is over at Jeff's house, as usual."

"Okay," said Manou. Karl spent a lot of time with Jeff's family. They were a regular American family and Manou supposed Karl liked their normalcy. If it helped him, it was fine with her. Sophia ran upstairs and slammed her door so that the thud echoed throughout the house. "And you two," Manou asked the others, "did you get a snack after school?"

They nodded.

"Why don't you go upstairs for the next half hour, too?"

They galloped up the stairs, too, Florence asking, "Francis, let's play Monopoly until dinner."

"After I go to the bathroom. I've had to go for..." The rest of Francis's answer was muffled as he went down the hall.

When the children were out of hearing range, Manou said, "Mutti, it's hard for the kids to think about Ernst."

Mutti slowly looked up at her, her eyebrows arched in a shock. "But they must! Or they will forget him."

"They will never forget him. He was their father. But his death was so sudden. They have been struggling to handle it. They are just starting a new school year and they need to be positive."

"I tried to ask Karl about the accident but he said he didn't know a thing. "

"He probably just doesn't want to talk about it. He knows."

"What does he know? Is there something you are not telling me?" Mutti's voice sounded desperately afraid.

"No, Mutti. I've told you everything I know."

"He was sick, you said. He never should have been on the roads."

"That's right. I think he was a bit feverish and didn't realize how bad the rain was when he went to the hospital."

"But why did he go to the hospital?"

Manou hesitated. Should she tell Mutti about the psychiatrist? No. It was confusing but a dead end in terms of understanding Ernst's state of mind. "He thought he needed medicine."

"If you had been home, he could have sent you. You should have taken a day off work."

Guilt rained over Manou, harder than the storm on the day of his death. Again, she held her tongue instead of lashing back at her mother-in-law. She simply agreed. "Yes, I should have stayed home." She turned and went to the kitchen to prepare omelets and toast for supper.

Manou began her teaching routine, the kids settled into their classes, and Mutti belabored the past every day. Perhaps she sensed a mystery surrounding Ernst's drowning; perhaps she was simply working through her sorrow. Almost every night, Manou heard her weeping in the dark.

I don't weep anymore, Manou realized. No, she simply sat with that taut feeling enshrouding her, knitting together bits and pieces of life with Mutti's charismatic son. Ernst inspired much devotion from women, and Manou had achieved the most unlikely things with him, even getting a graduate degree herself. But so often he left her alone to wrap up his extravagantly conceived projects. Even when he died, he left her to raise their kids. Manou slowly acknowledged the flaw in holding him on such a high pedestal, the flaw that damaged them both. For her, it prevented her from seeing his decline; for him, it meant...what? When it came to his interior domain, with the facts of his death puzzling beyond comprehension, questions popped up in Manou's dreams or on the edge of her disturbed sleep, something urged her to deepen the search and look below the tip of the iceberg into a realm where the smallest words were a clue, where a repeated behavior should have forecast an outcome, where religious precepts, long held expectations, family influence, spiritual experiences, childhood dreams or handicaps might have been a factor. She dove slowly, steadily, and inevitably into that murky realm.

Ciaccona

The Devil's Dance

In an earthquake, the ground on each side of the fault line moves, but in opposite directions. As Mutti released her anguish on the Feidler family, with each passing week she became more like her capable self; Manou absorbed Mutti's sorrow along with her own and slid down under the weight of it.

One Thursday afternoon in November, Manou opened the bottom drawer of her office desk to put away some files and a bottle rolled forward. It was a half-empty bottle of Johnnie Walker Scotch whiskey—Ernst's favorite. Manou's head began to pound. She knew Ernst had been drinking too much the last few months before he died, and this bottle was proof that it had gone beyond the two or three drinks every evening and more at parties. She pressed her forehead as if holding back the floodgates of blame, but it didn't work.

I should have seen this, she moaned inside. I should have known what was happening before it was too late. Why did he disappear into alcohol? Why was he always lashing out at me like a terrified dog? What was he afraid of that he was too proud to admit?

His detachment, she now understood, was a cry for help. Her detachment was her armor against his cold fear.

Manou looked at the clock. It was time for class—his class in his classroom. She maneuvered like a puppet on strings, moving through the hall as he had moved and feeling surrounded, as he must have felt. She walked along in a blur of bodies and contorting faces, imagining the outlines of footsteps he had taken the day before his death. He had left school abruptly and then come home in the afternoon complaining of flu. But it wasn't flu at all. It was the same swirling terror she felt now. Standing in front of her oblivious students, Manou began to sweat and tremble. She knew Ernst stood beside her with an awful and familiar look of disdain, saying, "You and I are one, Marie Madeleine. I couldn't go on; neither can you. You don't have the right after sixteen years together."

"What did you say, Madame Feidler?" asked a student in the front row.

Suddenly not knowing what was real and what was fantasy, Manou rushed out of the classroom in a panic, running through the halls to the nearest exit, fleeing her students, her papers, Ernst's bottle of whiskey, and his ghost. But could she avoid some truth in his words? Should she exit life along with him because he couldn't go on? And because she didn't see this, she had no right to go on either?

Manou sat in the car clutching the steering wheel. I didn't see. I didn't help. I abandoned you, Ernst, didn't I? Her head raced with recriminations until she hit the wheel and said out loud, "I need help." Manou took a deep breath, started the car, and drove to a nearby payphone. She called Dr. Tremont and told him what was happening. "Come to the office right away," he said with concern, but later, when she went into the examining room, he was smiling. "I was wondering how long you would hold on."

"I thought I was managing pretty well but...it all just caved in. So suddenly."

"Describe how you felt, please."

"I felt so dizzy, trembling, and almost feverish. Everything was a blur."

He touched her hand in sympathy. "Four children. A job. The shock. Your mother-in-law is here...difficult under the best of circumstances, I'm sure."

"No, no, she's very..."

"Manou, you can't take care of everyone. This was to be expected, and now it's time to take care of yourself. Who is your supervisor at Valley College?"

"Charles Reston."

"I'm going to call him and tell him..."

"Oh, please don't. I'll be fine."

"Nonsense. You need a leave of absence until after the holidays. There isn't a person at the college who will fault you, Manou. You need to rest." He placed his hand on her shoulder. "Rest, Manou. Do you hear me?"

Manou nodded, feeling a sense of grateful relief that someone else was taking charge. Dr. Tremont picked up the phone and called a psychiatrist in the building, briefly explaining Manou's situation. They scheduled an appointment for her that afternoon.

"Dr. Richardson will give you some medication to ease the stress as well as help you talk through your grief."

"I'm not sure. Ernst tried therapy but it didn't do much for him."

"You are not Ernst." Manou looked up at the tone of his voice. Dr. Tremont sounded very grave, as if he already knew about the voice agitating inside her. "Go upstairs, now. Third door on the left."

Manou left, grateful for Dr. Tremont's kindness but anxious about the psychiatrist. Would he drag things from her that would sear and scrape as he exhumed them from her subconscious? On the contrary, Dr. Richardson sat behind a large desk, disturbingly quiet, serious, superior, and detached. Oddly, his down-turned lips reminded Manou of the Mother Superior who disciplined her at Catholic school. Manou was always in trouble for flouting the rules, and she often ended up in front of a large desk like this one, awaiting judgment.

When Manou arrived home that evening, she already felt out of her body from exhaustion and the Elavil he'd prescribed. She saw herself from above being falsely cheerful with her children and Mutti. At the end of the evening, she took Mutti aside. "I'm taking a leave of absence from teaching until January."

Mutti gave her a fearful look. "Does that mean you won't need me?"

"No, no, I need you very much. More, actually. I went to the doctor today and he said I needed rest. I'm...I'm terribly exhausted."

Mutti sighed with relief. "I was afraid..." She straightened her shoulders. "Oh well, how shall we manage this?"

Manou paused. She hadn't thought it through, and the medication made it hard to put her mind in any order. "I need to rest during the day. I need to be with the kids before and after school."

Now that Mutti realized she wouldn't be sent away—perhaps to her own lonely hell—she looked at Manou with softer, almost compassionate eyes. "Why don't you rest now and I'll take care of the children tonight. We can work out some kind of new schedule tomorrow." She gestured toward the stairs. Manou accepted the offer gratefully, especially because the Elavil made her feel so strange and she needed to lie down.

Manou returned the next week to Dr. Richardson. He asked for the details about the day of the accident and he recorded the conversations. It was very dry and boring. She had been over this a hundred times.

"I called him from work about 10 a.m."

"And how do you feel about that, Mrs. Feidler?"

"I thought he had the flu."

"And then what did your husband do?"

"He called our doctor."

"And how do you feel about that, Mrs. Feidler?"

"I didn't know about it at the time. I wish Dr. Tremont had been able to see him."

"And then what did your husband do?" It was all so perfunctory and all about Ernst.

It became more and more evident with each fruitless question that Richardson was not the person to share her fears and passions, to empathize with her profound loneliness, nor to help her discover why love had disintegrated before her very eyes without her acknowledgment. I'll do better on my own, she decided.

Before Manou left the reception room, she quietly leaned down and told the secretary, "Please cancel my next appointment. I won't be able to make it." The secretary did not look surprised or interested; she just opened her book to the next week and crossed out Mrs. Feidler. Without telling Dr. Tremont, Manou cancelled all her appointments and threw away her prescription. By doing so, she hoped to open her emotional fists and unlock the gates that confined her whole history with Ernst. Without the numbing tranquilizer, her body and mind reeled. During the day, she lay in bed, huddled in the fetal position, straddling madness and reality. Terrifying dreams beset her: she sank into quicksand, got lost in caves, fell into a bottomless abyss, fled from terrifying wild animals. She would wake up in a sweat. One night she ran gagging to the bathroom because she had dreamed she was swimming in a pool filled with excrement. The most terrifying nightmare, one that came again and again, was in a deep well where Ernst was calling, "Come...Come with me." Manou swam down into the water toward him, almost touching his outstretched hand, and then rushed back to the surface with her lungs screeching for breath. She didn't look back but knew he was pursuing her. She swam harder and lunged out of the well. Then she ran through a dark forest to the sea, and threw herself into the embracing waves, breathing deeply the musky, salty air.

"Why did you want to take me with you?" she asked the Ernst of her nightmare. "Nothing I did was ever good enough."

"You were a slut. A sinner, Marie Madeleine," answered his voice from the dark.

Manou's body surged from terror to anger, recollecting this old, old accusation. She jerked up in bed and snapped on the light. It was three in the morning. She did not want to sleep again, to drown in a canal, a well, or in the insane loops of her subconscious mind. She sat up and looked around the room for a lifeline. The tape player sat on her bureau. She had listened to Pachelbel's Canon all afternoon, soothed by the hypnotic repetition of its simple chord progression uncluttered by counterpoints, digressions, and diversions. There was enough of that in her own mind. She loved Baroque music, and in one of their wonderful conversations about composers and sonatas and symphonies on the road to California, Ernst had told her that the word baroque meant "irregularly shaped pearl." Like you, he had said, and me.

Manou smiled. And I am still proud to be unlike all the rest. That assertion settled her thoughts because it reminded her of what they once shared. It was a thread leading to calm.

Manou walked to the bureau in her bare feet and selected Air on a G String, part of Bach's Suite No. 3. While the intensity of the Partita reflected Ernst's spirit in the key of D minor, Manou needed the delicacy of the Canon and Air, both in D major. As she lay back on her rumpled sheets, the hint of longing in the notes made her sob. For the rest of the long night, she wept softly from the pit of her being, for Ernst, for her children, for herself, and for the inability of humans to truly know each other. Her sorrowing heart took her to the most unbearable depths and, with the strings of the violin, soared to the most sublime pinnacles. Over the weeks, the Air, the Canon, Albinoni's Adagio, pieces by Handel, Vivaldi, and other Baroque composers, would take her to that special place where music is not body or mind or spirit, but all of those and something more, something on the precipice of the senses. It is a form of kindness. It is peace. It is joy.

The music wrested Manou's soul back from the brink many times. The mellow compositions inspired memories of childhood that also gave her peace. She imagined lying on the fresh cut hay at La Bâtie. It was warm. A bee softly hummed around a blue cornflower. She entered the soul of herself as a child. She became the bee, the flower, and the scent of hay on a warm summer day. She was all of that, in the place where she had felt the most freedom, and she felt better.

Each day, as she walked the tightrope of madness, she also imagined collecting the broken shards of her disintegrated self. Manou knew in every cell of her body that at the end of his life Ernst had felt the same disintegration. The difference between them was that Manou wanted to put her pieces back together into a whole vessel, however imperfect and scarred it might be. Ernst had let his scatter into the water of Danville Creek along Highway 680.

By December, Manou felt almost ready to go back to the classroom. Her fear was that the fragile balance she had achieved, through her rest, music, and visualizations, would crumble if she relived the moment of her panic. She thought and thought about how she might prevent a repeat of that awful moment when she felt like a puppet being drawn to death. She thought about what Ernst had done best in the classroom. Where had his genius manifest most significantly. Perhaps, she thought, there is some way he can help me rather than drag me down. His biggest achievement was in the use of recordings to help students improve language pronunciation and comprehension. She realized she could use recordings in her classroom, too, in her own way. If she started to sweat and tremble and was unable to speak, she would turn on the recorder and the students could listen to their own voices.

Very pale and shaky, she went into her office a few days later. It is mine not Ernst's, she said to herself. Then she walked down the halls to the classroom, greeting students to keep her from seeing Ernst's shadow.

Finally, she entered her classroom and set the tape recorder on her desk. Okay. She breathed. Everything is going to be fine. And the first class went by without so much as a flicker of panic. So did the next three.

Manou went home that afternoon realizing she had a strength that she had never before known she possessed, and that it was all hers. She no longer needed Ernst Feidler, but she knew she did need help finding her whole self.

♪

When the Feidler family returned from Europe in 1959, they rented a suburban house in Pleasant Hill and Ernst began teaching at Valley College. Manou resumed her fitness classes. On the one hand, they resembled the typical American nuclear family: two boys, two girls, Dad worked, Mom was home during the day for the children, and they made payments on a station wagon. They had come far from their uncertain beginnings in Los Angeles, but they were restless, energetic souls ready for more. For Manou "more" meant going back to school in Berkeley to get a master's degree in French so she could teach, too. A friend had told her about the magical new birth control pills and Manou rushed to her gynecologist to get some. Her time of confinement with little children had an end in sight. For Ernst "more" meant taking on evening classes and playing violin at every opportunity.

Playing with the Chamber, Ernst had made a name for himself in the area, and in 1961, through his friend Dimitri Komarov, a Russian who was studying at the college, he was asked to perform a piece of his choice for a special Easter Sunday performance at the Our Lady of Kazan Russian Orthodox Church in San Francisco. It was a moment he had waited for since his days playing with John Lund in Iowa. He chose Bach's fifth movement of the Partita in D Minor, the complex Ciaconna he had played for Manou in the Wyoming desert seven years earlier.

Mutti returned for the winter and promptly lamented Ernst's heavy schedule. Nonetheless she continued to demand reverence for Ernst's practice time, expecting the children and Manou to be absolutely silent until the whole family knew every note of Ernst's Ciaconna by heart. He practiced diligently every night asking Manou about nuances of his interpretation of a piece of music considered one of the longest, most difficult compositions for solo violin ever written.

He would play a harmonic progression. "Manou, do you hear the theme? It is repeated again. Like this..." And he played the beginning and then one of the variations. "Hear it?"

"Yes, yes. I can," Manou replied from the sofa where she knit persistently in order to do more that just listen to the repetitions of his practice.

"But do you hear the continuous baseline?"

"What exactly do you mean?"

He played several bars. "The Ciaconna style was part of the finale of French ballets because this baseline unified the dancers and the performance." He played again and then rested his violin against his chest. "I think of the counterpoints as different voices, each asking something special of the musician, of me." He paused. "There are thirty-four variations. I hope I can hear them all," he added, and then picked up his violin and played from the beginning again.

Manou listened and listened, but it was not a piece of music she particularly cared for. The voices didn't sound distinct enough and she couldn't find the subtleties in his practice. She felt guilty about not deeply comprehending the composition that charmed all great violinists, yet she hoped Ernst mostly needed approval and attention from her. She understood that Ernst could taste success, ached for a music career after this performance, and felt his dream was finally about to come true.

Through February, March, and April he worked at his interpretation like a diamond cutter chiseling his jewel. As Easter Sunday approached, the kids became very excited to hear their father perform but Mutti became more and more nervous about the performance. She listened to Ernst's practice without her normal little smile of bliss and her hands sat still on her knitting. On Easter Sunday morning, she said she wasn't feeling well and would stay home, but she helped dress the kids in matching blue sweaters that Maman had sent from France in honor of the event. Mutti waved weakly from the porch as the Feidlers left for San Francisco in their Ford station wagon, Ernst whistling and tapping his fingers on the steering wheel.

"How are you feeling about this, Ernst? Nervous?" Manou asked him quietly.

"Not at all. Absolutely fine," he replied.

"Good. I know you'll be wonderful."

The road paraded before them, from Pleasant Hill through the Caldecott Tunnel and across the Golden Gate Bridge to San Francisco. The kids quibbled over a card game, but Manou and Ernst sat lost in their thoughts, their individual dreams. Manou felt a fist in her stomach. She looked at him but he seemed relaxed. I have more stage fright than Ernst does, she marveled.

The church was filled to capacity; the audience dressed in cheerful Easter colors, children carrying little baskets with beautifully decorated eggs. Ernst sat with the choir, looking around, lost in a world of his own. The family sat in the first row next to the bishops. Karl nudged Francis and pointed at the bishops' funny long beards and towering headscarves. Sophia made a face that looked long and sour like the cleric next to her brother and the others burst out giggling. "Shush," Manou warned them. "The service is about to begin."

A Russian Orthodox service is long, somber, and complicated under the lightest of circumstances, and the Resurrection of Christ was not a light circumstance for this venerable sect. After the Invocation, various readings, and incantations, the choir sang with operatic intensity. Then it was time for Ernst's performance. The Ciaconna was about fifteen minutes long, and the audience listened attentively to the detours of the musical phrases for about five minutes. Soon Manou heard shuffling behind her; she saw some children in the aisle. She looked over at her own kids, who knew every note by heart. Karl was whistling along silently. Sophia was swinging her feet, lost in other thoughts. Florence and Francis were kneeling between the pews playing a clandestine game of Rock, Scissors, Paper with their little fists. As long as they were quiet, Manou didn't care. The people behind her rustled their programs and coughed. She closed her eyes and silently begged time to move faster as the variations of the Ciaconna led up a sinuous musical road, promising a summit at every turn, only to begin a climb to the next summit, and the next, and the next. For Baroque enthusiasts the variations were undoubtedly intriguing. For ordinary folk, they were perhaps too esoteric to be interesting. Or maybe families just wanted to get home for Easter dinner. One of the bishops fell asleep and leaned his head on Karl's shoulder. Apparently few were familiar with this great piece of music or perhaps most had been hoping for a delicate interlude in the midst of the somber orthodoxy. Manou felt the waves of impatience and boredom swell behind her.

For whatever reason, Ernst's playing did not gain the attention or trust of the audience. Whereas normally he swayed and moved with the tides of the Ciaconna, easily drawing any observer into his passion, now he stood stiffly and played mechanically. Ernst's eyes were focused on his instrument, so she didn't know if he was impervious or in a state of grace. When the final notes reached their crescendo and Ernst put down his instrument, there was a collective sigh from the audience. He might have interpreted that sigh as praise, such as the sigh from an audience after an evocative line of poetry. Or he might have heard it for what it was: a simple sigh of relief.

In the church's community room, the buffet table was full of traditional Easter treats. The classic kulich was full of candied fruit, almonds, and raisins, and after the service, the Feidlers stood over their kids to keep them from stuffing too much pastry in their cheeks.

"How was the performance?" Ernst asked Manou in a whisper, as he pulled Florence's hand back from grabbing another piece of kulich.

"You played beautifully," she lied.

A bishop came over to shake his hand and thank him. "Such a difficult piece. The Sarabanda is a little easier, don't you think?"

"A fine effort, Ernst," said Dimitri, but his wife was tugging at his sleeve to go home so he shrugged apologetically as they left. "I'll see you at school."

After a few other lukewarm greetings and expressions of appreciation, Manou drove them back down the coast. Ernst was tired but they had promised Sophia that they would stop at the beach in Santa Cruz on the way home. Ernst did not even get out of the car as Manou went out on the sand to play with the kids. Later they went to the boardwalk and ate hotdogs for supper. While the kids roared by on the famous roller coaster, Manou looked at Ernst's face bathed in orange light. He looked so sad it made her hurt inside, but if she acknowledged his look, her recognition of his sense of failure, it would be an admission that the performance was good but not great. She couldn't do that to him.

Mutti was asleep when they got home. The next morning she asked how it had gone. "It was beautiful," Manou responded immediately.

Mutti turned to ask her son. "Yes? Ernst?"

He paused a moment and said, "You know what, Mutti? I've been thinking about coming back to Germany."

"Oh, I would love that, my son." Mutti smiled and patted his hand. She didn't ask anything else about the performance.

Manou was stunned. He had said nothing about this to her. "This is sudden."

"America is a land of mirages," he continued. "Everything is new, no substance, no history."

The girls chattered about *Charlotte's Web*. Karl raced a little car across the table and it clattered into a glass.

Abruptly, Ernst stood up and grabbed the car and grabbed his son by the wrist. "How many times have we told you no toys on the table during meals? Go to your room." Karl looked like he was going to cry but he bit his lip and ran up the stairs. The girls sat looking puzzled by their father's outburst. "And you two stop gibbering about a silly little pig."

Sophia put her cereal spoon down. "May we be excused?" she asked barely above a whisper.

"Go. Get ready for school and be waiting at the door for me in ten minutes."

The girls raced upstairs, too. Francis got up and went to sit in Mutti's lap.

Upstairs, as Manou and Ernst were dressing for work, she said, "I don't think you needed to be so hard on Karl and the girls."

"Oh no?" Ernst turned to her, color rising from his cheeks to his forehead. "I get to decide how to discipline my own children. I work two jobs and go to school, to feed five insatiable mouths. How dare you tell me how to respond to them. If it weren't for you, I wouldn't even be in this shallow, greedy country. I'd be someplace that appreciates my art, someplace I could play music exclusively instead of haphazardly in the midst of this mad dash for money, money, money."

"I'm so sorry you feel like this. I'll try...." Her words felt clumsy, weak. She suspected this was fallout in the aftermath of the performance.

Ernst stomped over to her, his faced redder than before. "You all are nothing but a ball and chain locked to my feet. I'm a prisoner." He grabbed his suit jacket from a hanger. "I never would have married you if I'd known I was going to get stuck in this country."

He jammed his wallet in his back pocket. "And then you were no virgin when I married you. Remember?"

"Ah, my virginity, again."

"Marrying you was an act of charity. And you took advantage of me."

Manou almost didn't recognize his face because it was so contorted in anger. She recoiled against the closet door and began to cry. "Ernst, I never meant to force you to do anything, you know. Just tell me how I can make it up to you."

"You can't," he said as he left the bedroom.

Manou went through her day berating herself, trying to think of ways to appease him and to bury the truth of his poor execution of the Ciaconna. Yes, this country did not support artists. Yes, she was the "bad girl." It was not his failure; it was hers that she couldn't make more time for his practice. That evening, he was sullen when he returned home. Manou distracted the children and prepared Ernst's favorite *coq au vin*. Good food usually softened his moods, yet even though he cleaned his plate, he remained morose. Mutti placed his violin on the table after dinner as she always did. He stared at it and said, "I'm not playing tonight." He sat in the armchair with a Scotch and water, and after Mutti quietly put the instrument away, she filled a pan of warm water and sat at his feet to perform her ritual cleansing.

Ernst only practiced once that week, and the following weekend he took his kids on an outing as he did every Saturday. They all returned covered in sand, smelling like the Pacific Ocean and sun, and even Ernst was now in hearty spirits. On Sunday night, he lay in bed and stared at the ceiling while Manou read. As she reached to turn out her light, he stated simply, "Let's build another house. Just for us. Not to sell."

Manou was silent, remembering how much she had shouldered the responsibility building the duplex when he was busy, even though she was pregnant. "With me going to school, I really would only be able to work in the evenings."

"I know. But we can start in the summer when we can work all day. You'll get your degree at the end of May, and then when you teach full time in the fall, we'll have two incomes. It will all be more affordable."

"Why now, Ernst? We're so busy."

He held up his hands and turned them one side to the other, first looking at his palms, then his fingers, then slowly clenching and unclenching his fists. "See these? Now I can damage them. It doesn't matter anymore." Before she could respond, he flashed his beautiful smile at her. "Come on, Manou. Let's build a house."

She melted again.

The house project was an enormous one. By the time they added all the amenities they wanted for their big family, the architectural plans called for a 2,800 square foot two-story, six bedroom home. They duplicated the process that had worked so well in Pacific Grove. They made a down payment on a lot, subdivided it and sold half, applied for a building permit, subcontracted the concrete work, plumbing, and electrical, and did the carpentry themselves. They poured the foundation with Mutti and the kids watching from a picnic blanket on the hillside above the lot. Over the summer, Ernst and Manou got to the site at daybreak and worked until sunset. In the fall, Ernst went back to his teaching schedule and told the Chamber that he didn't have time to play with them anymore. Manou got a job teaching morning classes at Contra Costa High School even though she'd postponed writing her thesis until after the house was finished. At noon, she picked Francis up at kindergarten and set him up to play with wood scraps in the yard while she hung doors and painted trim.

Manou listened diligently to the news of the day as she worked on the house. The previous year, Manou had been enthralled by the campaign and election of John Kennedy although Ernst was more conservative. She had wanted to vote for Kennedy but when it came time to actually cast her ballot, at the last minute she voted for Nixon, her husband's preference. As she left the polling booth, she felt mystified at herself. Why hadn't she voted for her own preference? Out of guilt? Out of respect for her husband? Why? When the Freedom Riders were attacked in Alabama, she applauded Robert Kennedy's efforts to protect them against the onslaught of the Ku Klux Klan. Ernst disagreed, saying the southern states should be able to make their own rules. "This is not many little fiefdoms, like the European continent," she replied. "It is one country that ought to have the same rules of fairness in each state." She felt better that she had stood up for her beliefs, at least in conversation. By August when they were framing the roof, Mutti's sister called to tell them the East Germans were building a wall in Berlin to control the refugees and there were American troops in Hof because it was so close to the border between East and West. President Kennedy advised Americans to create backyard bomb shelters because of the Cold War threat of the Soviet Union, but Manou and Ernst agreed that they would not live life in such fear. And so the tides of sameness and difference flowed between them, creating moments of harmony but, more often, moments of subdued friction.

The family moved in over Thanksgiving vacation. It was a gorgeous house, nestled into a hillside with an unobstructed view of Mount Diablo. The living room had an open beam ceiling and a black Swedish fireplace in the center. The bedrooms were full of light. They built a large playroom in the basement, and a sundeck the length of the house overlooked the backyard.

After the building was complete, Ernst and Manou passed each other like birds in flight as they pressed on with a flurry of new obligations. There was never empty space or time. When there was no more detail work to do on the house, Manou wrote her thesis. When Ernst finished the deck, he added another evening class. After the New Year, she taught full time.

Ernst stopped playing music completely and focused on methods of teaching language. He experimented with the new science of biofeedback. He recorded students' voices and compared their diction to sound waves of the same phrase stated with perfect pronunciation. They could actually see when they weren't perfect. His colleagues considered his method inventive, groundbreaking, and even "brilliant." The accolades didn't seem to make him proud, though. If anything, he seemed more critical of himself and more cynical than ever. He made bitter jokes and berated Manou for small transgressions.

For her own sense of quiet and peace in the hubbub of their life, Manou became a relentless knitter, finding quiet hours in their living room to become absorbed in the texture of yarn, the unfolding of intricate patterns. She knit as much as she had that winter in Marraine's apartment, waiting for the birth of her firstborn and the return of her lover. In spite of the beautiful sweaters she made for the whole family, Ernst would walk in the room and grumble, "Aren't you leading the life of leisure. Don't we all wish we had nothing better to do than sit and knit like a grandmother."

Every time he sneered at something she did, she ignored his hostility but added a skein of anger to her own basket of unexpressed resentment. Without acknowledging the prickling irritation inside herself, she looked for a way to knit her paybacks into their life in such a way that he couldn't get mad. She recalled something Maman had done every year to irk Papa with a creative flare: April Fool's Day jokes. So each year Manou schemed for just the right joke in response to Ernst's jabs.

April 1, 1963, irritated because he always acted so superior when she tried to discuss her teaching, she told him he had been named Teacher of Year—very plausible because students flocked to his classes inspired by his European charm, melodious voice, and inventive ways to teach foreign languages. She said he had to dress nicely because reporters were coming to interview him. He fussed over which suit to wear and slicked back his hair. Then he sat waiting in the living room, getting more and more nervous, until she finally burst into laughter and yelled, "April Fools!" He stared hard at her and then said, "Oh well, I did have an article written in the Valley paper about my biofeedback strategy."

April 1, 1964, after she had seen him flirt with a young woman at a party on their sundeck, she enlisted the help of one of his teaching colleagues. The friend told him that a beautiful blonde transfer student from Germany was dying to meet him. A rendezvous was arranged at the Red Lantern, a local bar. Ernst showed up for the date—and so did Manou, calling out, "April Fools!" as she sat on a barstool beside him. Ernst had a hard time getting mad about that.

April 1, 1965, because their intimacy was getting less and less frequent, Manou sent him an anonymous letter claiming that "his wife" was having an affair and that she met her lover every Thursday after school. Manou arrived late Thursday night and Ernst coldly asked, "Where have you been?"

"Oh, out."

"I know what you're up to."

Suppressing a laugh, Manou answered, "Really? Have you checked the calendar today?"

"What do you mean?" He looked at the calendar in the kitchen. "Oh no. Not again!" he yelled and stormed off until he cooled down. It did not help their love life.

Their opportunities for communication and reconnection as a couple evaporated as the small antipathies piled up. Ernst had a habit of springing guests on her, as if he often didn't want to come home and simply be with his family. Once he called her when she was home sick with strep throat and announced he'd be bringing his students home for a late dinner after night class. Manou protested. She couldn't prepare a meal; she was sick. He said, "Nonsense. What are you going to do? Stay in bed all day? You can get up long enough to set the table and make something good." And he hung up.

Manou was so furious that she ruminated for hours about what to do. At four in the afternoon, she threw on some old clothes, went to a boutique in Pleasant Hill, and bought a very expensive and provocative negligee. When the students and Ernst arrived about 9 o'clock that night, she answered the door wearing only her negligee. "I'm so sorry but I'm not well this evening. I won't be joining you but you'll find ingredients for a meal on the kitchen counter." She slinked up the stairs to bed. Ernst got the point and began to give her better warning about visitors, but he still wanted an overzealous social life.

During the school year, they were like the two sides of a marital fault line, moving in opposing directions, constantly shaking the terrain of their lost passion for each other. The only respite from the tension came in the summer. Since they were both teachers they had a couple of months of vacation, and they pursued the pleasure that had attracted them to each other in the beginning: romping in the great outdoors. They loaded the kids into a camper and pulled a boat up to Mount Shasta. They camped at various lakes to fish and hike and water ski with their kids. Ernst left his pressures behind and gave his family all his attention. When Mutti was with them, they would take off alone to rekindle their sense of belonging together. Their favorite place was Chilnualna Falls, a series of waterfalls about 700 feet high in the southern section of Yosemite National Park. The falls fell in cascading tiers and Ernst and Manou climbed the twisting, turning switchbacks with the exhilaration they had felt years ago back on the buffs overlooking the Iowa River. On the way down, they took a detour to a favorite hidden pool where they rediscovered the warmth of their bodies in the cool water of the creek.

Yet, when the school year resumed, so did their friction. Their obligations drew them away from the gorgeous house on the hill as much as the constancy of raising the kids allowed. They loved being with their children, and they spared them their underlying tensions by never openly acknowledging conflict to each other. When spats arose, they circled each other like suspicious dogs then turned and went in opposite directions. Ernst took the kids on adventures every weekend—fishing, clam digging, and beach combing. When they came back, Manou had cleaned the house, corrected her papers, washed the clothes, knitted, and cooked a delicious French meal. When Ernst didn't have weeknight classes, she had late meetings at school.

As their distance grew and grew each year, Manou reached out for friendships and took up skiing with a passion. Winter weekends, she went to Squaw Valley with Lucy when the lifts opened in the morning and they skied until the lifts closed. She came home feeling the old confidence and satisfied exhaustion of athletic accomplishment. Manou even went to France alone one summer leaving the family in Mutti's care.

As she became more independent, Ernst seemed to wallow in ailments that came and went but demanded much attention. First, his old thyroid problem acted up. The doctors were able to treat it with medication. Then he had a series of midnight panic attacks. He'd awaken from nightmares, his chest constricting in excruciating pain, calling out, "Leave me alone!" Manou had no idea who he was yelling at in his dream but she rushed him to the emergency room. They returned with just a few tablets of Valium and an admonishment to rest.

Then the old fencing scar on his cheek inexplicably swelled and pulsed feverishly. After extensive testing, he was diagnosed, respectively, with tuberculosis, cancer, and sarcoidosis. Ernst hated the medications so much that the pills invariably ended up in the garbage. A student had suggested jogging might help his lungs so he starting jogging every day. It worked. The swelling and the blurry spots on his lung X-rays cleared up, and he quit his short-lived habit.

None of this encouraged Ernst to slow down his daily pace. One morning Ernst announced, "I've registered at UC Berkeley."

"For what?" Manou asked. "You've already got a BA in French and Russian and an MA in music."

"I want to get a PhD in Educational Psychology and continue my experiments in language acquisition. I think I'm really on to something with my pronunciation device." His jaw was taut, letting her know there was no argument.

Manou sighed with bottomless weariness at their pattern of endless dissatisfaction. "Of course. You will make a huge contribution, I know."

Having received her benediction, he softened. "I thought that before I start the program in the fall we could go to Yosemite again."

This was a true and rare olive branch of peace. Manou smiled and said, "I would love that so much, Ernst. To Chilnualna Falls? Just the two of us?" She was offering the branch back to him. He smiled almost shyly with the memory, and then turned quickly away. "Yes."

The opening was enough to give her hope, hope that the previous difficult months had been a variation on the theme of their marriage, like a variation in the Ciaconna that came to a harmonic end.

♪

Manou recovered from her breakdown over the winter of 1970. Her new emotional beginnings created switchbacks between tension and release, trepidation and elation, and each realization demanded deeper exploration. Mutti's six-month stay ended and she left, taking with her the pointed finger of guilt. Although she had rallied to help while Manou rested, she still had flung little darts tipped with poison. She muttered phrases such as "If he'd only stayed in Germany," or "Ernst never would have let Karl do that," or "You should take better care of Francis." Manou went through exhausting rounds of self-recrimination and recovery.

After dropping her mother-in-law at the airport, Manou opened all the car windows and let the delicious California spring air rush in. For the first time in a year, in spite of the approaching anniversary of Ernst's death, Manou felt alive. She was forty years old and felt a new start embedded in this rush of ocean breeze. Now that her emotions were on even ground, she admitted to herself that she had reacted daily to the charisma of Ernst, not the substance, because he had exuded the impression of strength in every endeavor except one violin performance. When Manou shook him down off this pedestal, though, she saw that he had been floundering. He wasn't strong; he was driven. He never felt triumphant in his profession; he felt insecure. He wasn't completely happy, ever; and neither was she. She always had followed his lead and it made her mad at herself. How could I have been so blind? she asked, her exuberance turning to fury. I called it love but it was just a recreation of Mutti's, her mother's, and grandmother's relationship to men. She may not have washed his feet literally but she engaged in an insidious slavery to him nonetheless.

Back at home, she found herself pounding pillows again, thrashing the water in the pool, and storming around her room in a rage. She had pretended their problems were the exception not the rule for sixteen years. Now that she had opened Pandora's reality box it couldn't be shut.

Manou chronically felt like an anxious snake slithering around truth. She wanted to know it, be done with it, and find serenity. Not with the over-optimism of the Méthode Coué. Not hiding behind work and family. She wanted to know Manou. Her experience with psychiatry had been a bust, but it was 1970 and she lived in California, the heart of revolutions in political, sexual, culinary, drug, and psychological cultures. She had seen it manifest in her students since she returned to California in 1961, in their bright rag-tag clothing, their scruffy appearance, the slight scent of marijuana smoke when they entered the classroom, but more positively, in their unwillingness to take the status quo for granted. They reminded Manou of herself in Catholic school, where bending the rules and getting reprimanded just made her more resistant.

There was a smorgasbord of new values, new therapeutic options to discover and redefine one's self. Manou wanted to sort out the charlatans from the new visionaries so she took a rather academic approach to finding the right therapy for herself. She read books, magazines, and newspapers about the new choices. The Human Potential Movement appealed to her because of its origins in the existentialism of her youth and because it emphasized body awareness. Then there was Eric Berne's Transactional Analysis that focused on patterns of transactions that popped up repeatedly in everyday life. He called them games, which resembled the interpersonal knots Manou and Ernst got caught up in. But she didn't want to endlessly dissect what had happened with Ernst. She wanted to rediscover her self. This led her to consider Fritz Perl's Gestalt Therapy out at the Eselen Institute in Big Sur. But encounter groups often involved hot tubs, hallucinogens, Eastern religions, or group massage—not Manou's style. Finally, she hit upon Psychosynthesis, which began before and informed the alternatives of HPM, TA, and Gestalt. Since she felt splintered and unable to find her core after giving it over to Ernst for so many years, she choose this process in which the focus was to bring together the divergent parts of the personality.

With Dr. Elaine Vincent, Manou started spreading out the puzzle pieces shaped from the pain of her marriage, her denial of emotional reality, the anger of discoveries, and the sighs of acceptance. Intense emotions and encrusted ideas revealed themselves in many different ways in the sessions: simpering, explaining, arguing, disguising, denying, crying, justifying, excusing, or triumphing. They came without order from her guts, breaking through an intense censorship of her mind and disordered words. Dr. Vincent gently pushed her until the mind opened and the words fell into place.

In a session, she suggested that several characters manipulated Manou.

Manou bristled. "That's not true. You're wrong. It's just me."

"Who is that arguing with me?" Dr. Vincent asked. "Give her a name then eventually you can pull her strings like a puppet instead of her controlling you."

Manou sat back, intrigued by theatrics of this exercise. "Okay. She is... umm, let me think...Rosine."

"Tell me about her."

"Rosine is the pessimist...and a hypochondriac. She is anxious, embarrassed, and doesn't trust anybody."

"Why not?"

"She is afraid everybody is better than she is."

"What happens when she feels this way?"

"She gets sick, always with an imaginary incurable disease. Like malaria. Or cancer of the liver."

Slowly Manou identified a collection of puppet characters that influenced her behavior. Marie was sweet, submissive, and good. She accepted everything without complaining. Afraid of speaking for herself she followed blindly. "C'est la vie," she muttered with unassailable fatalism, anger seething beneath the surface. Antoinette was sensual and charming. She loved clothes and delicious food, and manipulated people into giving her these things, but she needed constant reassurance that she was beautiful. Lucie was the dictator, terribly critical, aggressive, and competitive. She always had something to prove. Sarah was an actress. Marguerite was efficient, organized, patient, and disciplined—boring but useful. When Manou got stuck in looking at her real life behaviors, Dr. Vincent referred to these personalities who played in the theater of her life. The synthesis emerged through Manou's recognition of their roles and interaction. Manou learned that she wasn't shackled to these personas; rather her consciousness could conjoin them and evolve. She visualized her increasing awareness unfolding on a stage:

Act One. Background: unconscious. The characters are formed at random, unaware of each other. Their interaction is instinctual. They confront life's circumstances as best they can but often create a malaise of disconnection. Curtain.

Act Two. Background: semiconscious. The characters begin to recognize each other. They know they exist but they are unable to mitigate each other's behavior yet. Their interaction still creates confusion. They need a director. Curtain.

Act Three. Background: a dim light. The director makes an entrance. None of the characters is thrown out of the play, rather they are placed in their proper place: stage left, stage right, center stage, or backstage. Curtain.

Fourth Act. Background: a brighter light.

Manou became an enlightened observer if not quite a confident director. She began to smile at Antoinette's manipulations, to reassure Rosine, and to encourage Marie. She did not judge them and took refuge in a character when she needed her. But the director and observer were always present, intervening with self-love, enlisting the positive aspect of each part of her psyche. She learned compassion for herself and Ernst, although she regretted that he never went through this process. She felt immense sadness that many characters had controlled his life, and he had succumbed to the one who loved him the least.

With Dr. Vincent, Manou recalled many moments. Moments adding up collectively to make a lifetime: moments of despair, moments in limbo, moments of ecstasy and joy. She saw her life as a pendulum of emotional experiences swinging back and forth, sometimes clanging ominously like an old grandfather clock, sometimes laughing like a child swinging on a rope over a creek. By releasing all those old experiences, she gained a measure of happiness for the present, when she could stay in a fraction of time, give it her full attention, forget her regret of the past and the portent of the future, and savor the instant without jumping into step, as she and Ernst had done every second of their shared life.

Her synthesis was episodic. Sometimes her engines of distress were quiet; sometimes all systems flowed. Sometimes she still raged, yet Manou began to experience wholeness for longer and longer moments.

One August night she lay awake at three in the morning. The air had hardly cooled but it blew the ficus leaves lightly outside the wide-open sliding door. The darkness shimmered with the breeze, too. She was completely still and a thought tiptoed into her mind. Where are you now, Ernst? Where is your soul? Have you met God?

Manou laughed quietly at her question. In the house at La Bâtie, Grand-mère had a big illustrated catechism. God was an old man with a white beard sitting on a throne floating on a cloud and surrounded by respectful cherubic angels. Underneath the image was the inscription "God sees everything, and he is everywhere." There were also horned goat-like devils with cloven hooves taking the damned toward a gaping hell. They were pushing the sinners into fire with great pleasure. Odette and Manou had been intrigued and petrified by the images. But generally, the family's Catholicism was a shallow affair. First Communions were pretexts for parties; nuns at the convent school were mean old biddies who took too much pleasure in spiteful discipline. If there was a shred of pleasure in service to God, it was not manifest in the Sisters of St Francis. Catholic education had been the coup de grâce for Manou's religious beliefs. After four years of their ineffectual imposition of morals on her, the Church signified childish ideas, malaise, and oppression. On the contrary, Existentialism pulsed with life, especially with her Parisian post-war university crowd. Manou loved the intellectual discussions and resonated with the notion that meaning in life was to be found in action, not in a deity as cartoonish as Zeus or Thor.

Now, all of a sudden, she was asking a spiritual question she hadn't bothered to ask for decades: What was God? If there was such a thing, it was certainly much, much deeper and richer than the old man in the catechism. Probably untouchable and indescribable. As she lay in the dark, Manou felt some untouchable, indescribable thing in her core that, for lack of a better word, she called a soul. It clearly had been buried deep under layer upon layer of habits, traumas, and fears. How marvelous it would be, she thought, to recover that thing deep inside her, to tap into it like into the nucleus of an atom. She concentrated on this idea, trying to peel away those layers between her conscious mind and this intuitive essence, imagining herself no longer as a collection of puppet characters but as the effortless energy of an atom.

As she reached into this subterranean part of herself, she began to experience a strange sensation: a force spread through her muscles, through her whole being, while she remained completely still and relaxed. It built up inside her and she abandoned herself to it. She felt so strong that she imagined herself lifting a mountain. Her body tingled with rapture, uplifted in joy, in the most intense emotion of love. She floated in bliss, in complete peace, feeling that nothing could ever hurt her. This is Spirit, she realized. This is my spiritual soul. The thought rushed through her veins: "I am not afraid of death."

And what of Ernst and the question that had inspired this rediscovery of a profound spirituality? Was his soul part of this rapture? She hoped so.

And then she went back to sleep.

When she awoke the following morning, she felt astoundingly happy, happier than she had ever felt before, and it lasted for days. She returned to earth with humor, using the tools of her psychosynthesis: Marguerite put the harness back on, scoffing at her sense of liberation; Rosine suggested her blood pressure was out of order and this accounted for her ecstasy; Antoinette was sure she was simply sexually frustrated and her experience was a "spiritual" orgasm. Lucie just laughed. But Angelina was beaming and confessed to initiating the search. It didn't matter what the fragmented pieces of her self claimed. Manou knew her soul was real. It was whole.

♫

Manou poured cream into the butternut squash bisque and stirred it slowly over the heat. A pear torte was baking in the oven. Karl was playing basketball; Sophia was at a Beth's house; Francis and Florence were in their rooms doing homework before dinner so they could watch

Star Trek. Ernst walked in the front door of the new house in Walnut Creek and dropped his briefcase on the hall chair.

"*Bonjour, mon chéri,*" Manou greeted him.

He went straight to the freezer and pulled out an ice tray. He popped some cubes into a glass, took it to the liquor cabinet, and poured himself a scotch-on-the-rocks. He ambled into the living, sat in his armchair, and took a drink. He leaned back heavily and closed his eyes.

"Did you have your methodology class today?" Manou called to him from the kitchen.

Ernst didn't answer so she went to the doorway between the living room and the kitchen. "Ernst?"

He opened his eyes.

"Ah, just checking to see if you are alive."

"I am. And yes I had my methodology class today."

Manou returned to stir the bisque but called back to him, "Principal Thomson wants to send me to a conference on teaching foreign languages next month. It's in LA. They are featuring some educators from Harvard and the University of Chicago. It should be fun."

"So now you think you are a big foreign language educator?"

Manou spun around at the loud sarcasm of his voice. He was standing by the kitchen table holding his empty glass.

"I am just glad to go to a conference for three days. It will be nice to get out of class. And yes, I do think I'm a pretty good high school instructor."

"It doesn't take much to teach fourteen-year-olds."

"Ernst, you could show me just a little respect, you know. I have my master's too."

He shrugged, poured himself a second drink, and walked into the living room. "Call me when dinner is ready."

Manou stood completely still. It had been this way since school started. They'd had a really nice summer at Lake Shasta. Ernst seemed healthier than he had been in a long time. They ate and slept outdoors, smelling the pines. They swam early in the morning in the chilly lake and roasted marshmallows over a big campfire at night. He acted almost flirtatious, like he loved her again. While the great outdoors was a pleasant narcotic, Manou also thought his high spirits were in part because he'd completed his PhD in Educational Psychology and was highly praised for his thesis.

Yet the fun was short lived. When they returned from vacation, they had moved into this house. Last spring, he had accepted her reasoning that the schools were better and it was closer for her to drive to Contra Costa High School to teach. Yet, since the day they sold the house they had built in Pleasant Hill, he'd begun to make bitter comments about the change.

In October, his colleagues had thrown him a party to celebrate his new degree. Ernst took a long time bathing and getting dressed, and they arrived late. They cheered heartily when Ernst walked in the door, but he looked away as if their compliments were embarrassing. After a drink and a quick plate of food from a buffet, he tugged Manou's sleeve and said he wanted to go home.

When they got in the car, Manou asked, "Why didn't you want to stay? The party was for you."

"My PhD doesn't really matter. I'm too old to succeed at anything now."

"Ernst," she exclaimed with utter disbelief, "you're only thirty-eight. You're just beginning. You are going to have a remarkable career."

"No, I won't."

The rest of the fall he had descended into this chronic sour frame of mind. When he wasn't distant and cold, he was spiteful and sarcastic. To Manou—not the children. Never the children. Ernst seemed his happiest when he was organizing them for their weekend ventures, and when he was home, he helped them with homework and projects.

After dinner, Francis and Florence went into the den to watch TV and Manou worked on a needlepoint project—a beautiful design of blue and white birds, gold leaves and tree branches, all born from an incandescent sun. Ernst had only moved from his armchair to the dinner table and back. She wanted to talk to him, to take advantage of their rare presence together in the house like this, but he was lethargic and impenetrable.

She sighed and put down her work. "I wish we could talk about something."

"I'm not interested in making small talk," he muttered.

"You seem so unhappy."

"Why? Just because I have nothing to say to you?"

That stung but she continued, "No, because you seem listless. I...I miss you when you are so distant. I just want to be... "

"I'm exhausted. I had a faculty senate meeting today. The blasted SPCA is trying to get us to stop the psychology experiments with white rats. Unbelievable. Those animals get fed the best food, have the best environments, and play in rat mazes every day. A little zap on the nose when they chose the wrong door isn't cruelty." He stood up abruptly. "There. I've talked."

"That's not exactly what I had in mind. If you won't tell me why you are so angry and withdrawn, why don't you talk to someone else about it?"

"You mean like a shrink?" He snorted with disgust at the very idea.

She picked up her needlepoint again, held it to her chest like it might provide a shield against his reply.

"Manou, you're the neurotic one. You go to a shrink." And he went upstairs to bed.

Upset and restless, Manou couldn't sleep. Every day she ran into the same wall. He wouldn't communicate. What could she do? She felt like one of his little rats getting zapped on the nose for choosing the wrong thing to say, the wrong thing to do. Maybe she should see a shrink. She imagined what an analyst would say about her and she had to laugh a little. Probably plenty. Maybe humor was the way to reach him. She sat down at the kitchen table and began to scribble boxes and connections that looked like a maze. When she was done she took a clean sheet of paper and wrote:

Mrs. F's Neurotic Condition
The Amazing Maze
By Dr. Von der Artz

Mrs. F. created the Amazing Maze with all possible solutions to her marital dilemma. Here is what the "rat" thinks. This maze has been created for Professor E. F. because the only language he understands is in the form of a diagram. Although the patient finds much humor in her approach to the Neurosis, she is very concerned Professor E. F. will give her a lower grade because it is not in essay form.

In our recent sessions, I had Mrs. F. explain the symptoms of her complicated marriage. The artificially created Neurosis of her Maze seems pretty helpless to me. I have examined the patient and found her to be sane and sound. I was hoping to pin the problems on some previous childhood experience (as was her husband) but have been unable to uncover this to date to explain her conflict between Reward and Punishment. In addition, she is very intelligent and startled me by her knowledge of psychology.

Although Solution #1 is the preferred remedy to this situation, it cannot be implemented for the following reasons:

Professor E.F. does not believe in therapy as a remedy to problems.

Professor E. F. has such a strong ego that it is impossible for him to admit he is wrong or to give in.

Professor E. F. actually likes a little neurotic atmosphere around him because it creates in him a feeling of superiority. He then becomes the strong one who tells others of their shortcomings.

The situation is not entirely bleak. Professor E. F. seems to love his wife and kids and I wish I could impress upon him the seriousness of this situation.

Well, chin up to the F. family

The Shrink

THE AMAZING FEIDLER MAZE

Start here:

The golden years of hope, happiness, and belief that love is the most wonderful thing, and that everything is possible. The patient accepts the self as described by her partner, though often degraded by him, in the hope he will eventually realize her real goodness and true person in time. In the meantime, the patient accepts his underestimation of her as just punishment. It seems to be his crusade.

Condition: Center of the Maze

Neurosis: Patient is aching for the love of her partner

Stimulus: Need for Change

Patient realizes she is not being recognized for her true value.
Rebels against passive acceptance.
Hope is lost that partner will realize these things himself.

Behavioral Variables:

#1   Partner finally gives complete acceptance

#2   Withdrawal

#3   Go to sleep for one hundred years like Sleeping Beauty

#4   Get a new partner

#5   Drop the need for change: Be a masochist

#6   Have a nervous breakdown

#7   I don't know what the hell else to do I give up

Outcome: Possible Responses from Partner

#1 **Punishment:** continued non-acceptance, disinterest, rejection, accusation

#2 **Reward:** new acceptance, love, happiness, trust

Manou re-read her creation. A little theatrical but fun, she thought. She folded it and left it on the table. At breakfast, she handed it to Ernst with a smile. "I thought you might get a laugh over this."

He gazed at it casually and stuffed it in his pocket. "I have to get to work," he said as he left the table. "I have a class tonight so I'll be home late."

"Well," she shrugged towards his empty seat, "At least my students love me."

While the kids dressed for school, she went upstairs and pulled on a beautiful royal blue blouse and black skirt, accenting them with a shimmering silk scarf she had found at a boutique in Walnut Creek. She gazed at her reflection in the full-length mirror. The woman who looked back at her would raise eyebrows on the streets of Paris. She laughed knowing she was merely going to teach at the local high school, but what the heck, it still was très amusant to see students sit up and take notice when she strolled into class like a model. At a PTA meeting, a parent of one of the girls had said, "Every evening Elaine tells me what gorgeous outfit you wore in class."

Manou also used other tricks to get attention. When class was unruly, she'd lean on the desk with a stunt she'd learned in gymnastics: She could levitate her body up on her elbows in a gravity-defying move. The students quieted, mouths open at her trick. Her ever alert students learned good language skills, even loved French, and often took a semester in France organized through the Alliance Française. Manou was proud of her work, even if Ernst was oblivious. Every day she did her best to fill the hole created by his distance, his arrogance, and rejection.

It was a gloomy December, rainy and cool for California. Lucy Carter invited the whole family to spend the first weekend of the month at her cabin in Boulder Creek in the Santa Cruz mountains. It was the holiday season and Manou had hoped the outing would resemble their family time spent at Mount Shasta, inspiring them to feel connected again, but instead Ernst drank a lot on Friday evening and woke up in a sour mood Saturday morning. The kids got up and went outside to explore right after breakfast. Lucy went out, too, to show them all her favorite spots on the San Lorenzo River. Manou finally persuaded Ernst to take a walk with her that afternoon. They found a path through the trees that went down to the shore of the river, and they stood there in silence. The fresh air and the murmuring water soothed Manou. She looked at Ernst, hoping it was having the same effect on him, only to find him staring over the river, scowling. He suddenly said, "I am too good to be taken away by this cold river."

"Come on, Ernst," she pleaded. "It's beautiful."

He shook his head. "You'll never understand."

"It's St. Nicholas Day. Can't we enjoy it. I've got some presents for the kids and," she began to say and softly touched his hand.

He jerked back from her touch, whirled, and headed back to the cabin.

The rest of the holidays were blanketed in a similar gloom. Ernst mostly sat in his armchair as if Christmas with his family was a sad obligation. Manou gave up trying to penetrate his frame of mind. When he didn't want to communicate, there was no forcing it. In the past, he had always turned his mood around on his own, only when Ernst Feidler was good and ready.

♫

Ernst awoke in a sweat. That putrid being infested his dream again. Snickering, calling, sticking out his vile tongue, gesturing with long fingernails that clicked as they curled and uncurled in a mocking invitation to come. But where?

Ernst got up and slipped out of bed so he wouldn't wake Manou. He tiptoed downstairs, turned on the overhead light, and helped himself to a slug of Scotch straight out of the bottle. It helped quell his fear, at least for a while. What really terrified him was that the creature had been only in his dreams until he returned from a visit to Mutti last summer. Then he had seen it in his waking hours, too, first along the highway and then at a window wherever he was, like the office, the bedroom, a store, or the car.

Mutti. She had suddenly aged so much. He saw it in Hof when she looked up from his foot massage. The lined face, hooded eyelids, gray hair, and bent body. She was sixty years old. She will die soon, he realized, and the thought felt like poison burning his veins. She had always been there for him. Who would take her place? Could he live without her in the world?

Maybe he should just go with the goat-man. Save himself, Mutti, Manou, everyone a lot of trouble. Why not? Ernst took another swig from the bottle. The liquor burned, too, but at least the aftermath would be numbness and, if he was lucky, sleep.

In the morning, he had a headache but a quick glance at Mount Diablo assured him that the goat-man wasn't at the window. He remembered that he had an early training session at the hypnosis laboratory at Stanford University where he was learning techniques to apply to his own specialty, foreign language learning. As part of his training, Ernst took Professor Sorenson's hypnotic susceptibility test, but he scored low, meaning he was not very hypnotizable. Now he had to take one hypnotic age regression session to see what it was like.

When he got to the lab, there were two graduate students preparing the room for his session. "Let's do it. I have to get back to Valley for class by eleven o'clock," Ernst said as he loosened his tie. Sam, who was studying for a PhD in Behavioral Psychology, was a new trainer. He was a bit uncertain so he planned to follow the protocol verbatim as written in Professor Sorenson's Manual of Hypnosis Practice. Another graduate student, Jeremy, was the observer.

"Don't worry if it doesn't work. I'm not very suggestible, you know." Sam leaned Ernst back in a comfortable chair.

"We know," Jeremy said, "but let's not worry about that. Just take this as an opportunity to relax, Professor Feidler." Jeremy sat on the table near the door and opened his notebook. He was the department's resident hippie. He pushed back his round wire-rim glasses and then pulled on his long mustache as he read his notes.

Sam turned down the lights and sat down next to Ernst. He opened the huge textbook and began reading slowly from the protocol:

"Take a nice deep breath and hold it. Now let it out and close your eyes. I'd like you to take your attention to your eyelids and the area around your eyes. Relax your eyelids so much that they just won't work. Now try to open them."

Ernst found that his eyes felt as heavy as when he was just coming out of sleep. He couldn't open them.

"Good, stop testing and go deeper. Send that feeling of relaxation down through your body, from the top of your head to the bottom of your feet."

"I'm going to do a check to make sure you have understood the instructions, and have been following directions. I'm going to lift your hand and drop it. Don't help me lift it. Helping me would remove the relaxation. Just let your arm be limp and relaxed."

With his eyes still closed, Ernst felt Sam lift his hand up and then let it drop down in his lap. Ernst moved his hand on his thigh.

"You'll do better with practice, so let's do that one more time and you will find that you can go even deeper. Take your attention to your eyelids and hold onto that relaxation. One more time, test them to make sure that they won't work. Good, stop testing and go deeper. Now send that feeling of relaxation that you are allowing in your eyelids down across your entire body, from the top of your head to the tips of your toes as if you meant to go ten times deeper. I'm going to lift your hand and drop it. Good."

Yes, it felt so good. He let go of the tensions that filled his limbs every day, the tensions the doctor said were probably from his old thyroid problem. But he was even having trouble holding onto this thought as his body felt almost asleep.

"Now let's relax your mind. Really allow your mind to relax like your body is relaxed. In a moment, I'm going to have you slowly and softly begin to count starting with the number one. After each number, let your mind double its relaxation. After a few numbers, it doesn't take long, you will be able to relax your mind so nicely that the numbers will fade away and disappear. Want that and you can have it very easily. When the numbers are gone, raise your right index finger to let me know. Begin...."

"One," Ernst said. He wanted this relaxation so much.

"Softer...Two"

"Two," Ernst whispered.

"Now double your mental relaxation. Three."

"Three." He didn't hear his own voice.

"Now let those numbers begin to fade away as you relax your mind."
Four.

"Double your mental relaxation and let the numbers fade away to nothing."

Five.

Nothing,

Nothing,

Nothing.

Ernst lifted his right finger. Sam was so quiet. Was he still there?

"In a moment I'm going to count from one to five. With each number that I count, I want you to relax so much that by the time I get to five you have doubled your relaxation.

"One. Relaxation is beginning to double.

"Two. Relax.

"Three. Relaxation is doubling throughout your entire body.

"Four. Relax.

"Five. The relaxation has completely doubled from the top of your head to tips of your toes."

Ernst experienced dark and quiet; somehow he knew he wasn't asleep.

"Ernst, you are now five years old. You are very small. Remember a day that was very important to you."

Beautiful bright lights fill Ernst's mind. He sees a huge tree spiraling upward, covered with lights. It is Altmarkt square in Plauen, where he grew up. The tree is surrounded by town houses and the fine Renaissance gable of the town hall is lined with candles.

"Who is with you?"

His little hand is holding Mutti's large hand, the one with her wedding band. They are walking through throngs of people in the Altmarkt, past countless stalls with festive wares shimmering in the gentle glow of the Christmas tree.

"Remember something very, very pleasant about this moment."

Something sweet and delicious fills his mouth. It is a bite of the Christmas stollen. He tastes dried fruit and almonds and licks the powdered sugar from his lips. He looks up. Oh Mutti, Look! Here he comes! Saint Nicholas!

"What did you say, Ernst? Jeremy, I think he's speaking in German."

Mutti laughs. "Oh, yes. There he is." But, Mutti, who is that behind him? Oh no, he is looking at me! His tongue, his tongue! It is so red. The claws are touching me! Help, Mutti! "Here, Ernst, don't cry. I'll pick you up and hold you." What is that horrible animal? "That is Krampus. He will punish the children who have been bad this year." But why is he chained to St. Nicholas? "That is so he can't beat little children and take them away to the woods." But Mutti, what if he breaks free? He will beat me and take me away. "Don't worry, *mein suesser*. St. Nicholas won't let him do that if you've been a good boy." Ernst fills with terror. He knows he has not always been good. He took sweets from the cupboard. He pretended to hide when Max was playing with him in the park. When Tante Ingrid came over, he refused to sing a song Mutti taught him. She had hit him with a wooden spoon for being so bad. He begins to sob harder.

"Don't cry, Ernst. I am going to slowly wake you up now. I am going to count down from ten...."

Ernst was now in the bathtub twisting and turning. Mutti was scrubbing him hard on his belly, his legs, his penis. It hurt. Stop. Stop. "I must clean you, son. We are all born in sin and must be cleansed." But I am good. You said so at the Altmarkt. "Yes, you are good for a little boy. St. Nicholas will bring you a present. But we are all bad in the eyes of God until we renounce the Devil." What does the devil look like, Mutti? "He looks like...well, he looks like Krampus." Ahh....

"Jeremy, go get Dr. Sorenson."

Little Ernst stopped screaming and writhing in the water. He stared at the apparition behind his mother with the horns of a goat, yellow eyes, and the long red tongue that snaked out of his mouth as he talked in a language Ernst couldn't understand. Ah, Mutti, there is the Krampus! What is he saying? He is coming for me! "Don't be silly. Now stand up and I'll dry you off." Don't leave me, Mutti. Don't turn out the light. He clutched her around the neck.

"Ernst, this is Dr. Sorenson. Let Sam go. You are going to take a breath deep into your chest."

Ahh... Ernst saw Krampus' sickening grimace open around his long slimy tongue.

"You are going to feel the breath reach all the way down to your toes and up to your head."

Yes. Dr. Sorenson's deep voice dimmed the image of Krampus.

"Now we are going to count backwards from ten. When we reach one you will wake up. You will not remember what you saw. You will feel good feelings. Now repeat after me. Ten."

Ten. Krampus was gone.

"Nine," said Sorenson.

"Nine," said Ernst.

They counted all the way back to one and Ernst awoke to the kind faces of Sam, Jeremy, and the professor. Sorenson asked him, "Did you experience yourself as a child, Dr. Feidler?"

"No," Ernst lied. He smiled. "I guess I really am not very suggestible."

"Were you asleep?" asked Sam.

"I don't know."

"Sam, he was probably dreaming. A completely different state of consciousness."

"I don't think he was sleeping," said Jeremy, frowning with concern.

Sorenson ignored him. "We'll all go over the session notes so next time you can keep your subject from drifting off like that."

Ernst laughed softly, "Yeah, I don't want my German students dozing off. They do enough of that already. But I have to get to class up in Pleasant Hill now so it'll have to wait."

Ten minutes later, Ernst sat in his car in the Stanford University parking lot. He took his suit jacket off because he had soaked his shirt with sweat. Now at least he knew the name of the goat-man who plagued him: Krampus. It didn't make Ernst feel any better that the demon was a Christmas trickster. Myths went deep. Apparitions meant something about good and bad, dark and light. Krampus was not light.

When Ernst walked into the lab the next morning, the other trainees surrounded a table. "Hi, Ernst," called Sam. "Take a look at this. The latest in relaxation mechanisms." When Sam stepped back, Ernst saw a flickering light leap out of a small black box.

"What's that supposed to do?"

"The flashing lights apparently can change your brain rhythms."

"Far out," said Jeremy, "William Burroughs's calls this the Dreammachine. I tried it last night and, man, I saw the universe flash before my eyes. No shit."

Sam snorted. "What were you on, brother?"

"Exactly what do you mean, Jeremy. Explain it to me," asked Ernst.

"Oh, right, you're Mr. Scientific Method. Stimulus, Variables, Outcomes, and Reliability. All that. Okay." He pulled a book out of his backpack with the cover in French: *Le Travail* by William Burroughs.

"I didn't know you read French."

Jeremy grinned. "I am a man of mystery, Dr. Feidler, like you." He paused and looked at Ernst with his eyebrows raised with curiosity, and then he began thumbing through his book. "Ah, here it is: 'Subjects report dazzling lights of unearthly brilliance and color...elaborate constructions of incredible intricacy build up from multidimensional mosaic into living fireballs like the mandalas of Eastern mysticism'...and so on. See?"

"So it induces hallucinations. How is that relaxing?"

Sam said, "I guess it depends on the frequency of the flicker. It will be highly individual. In the best of circumstances, a subject would be able to adjust the device for a desired state of mind."

"I know what state of mind I'd go for. Ecstasy!"

"Right, but you're a freak, Jeremy."

"I'll take that as a compliment."

"Anyway, Ernst, that's what Sorenson wants us to investigate."

"That's exactly what I want you to do." Everyone turned to see Sorenson in the doorway. He strode into the room like it was his own house. "I read that hogwash by Burroughs. Jeremy, remember that drug-addled novelists don't make great scientists. But I read W. Gray Walter's papers from the 1940s about how flicker or strobe can produce hypnotic states of profound relaxation. Imagine what that could do for the treatment of anxiety disorders and insomnia."

Ernst watched the light blink for a minute. "If that's true, it could help with the self-consciousness of conversation in a second language, too."

"I bet you're right, Feidler. Want to try it out? I've got four flicker-fusion boxes...The engineering department is making me six more with better frequency adapters. I'll check one out to Valley and we can draw up a protocol for the study. We'll use the experimental design you set up for the pronunciation biofeedback."

Ernst smiled. "I'd like that." They walked toward the door.

Jeremy called out. "Watch what you catch with the Dreammachine, Dr. Feidler."

Ernst took the device home that night instead of leaving it at the college. He hooked it up in the bedroom and, ignoring Manou's protest, turned it on for a half hour before bed. He slept well so he tried it every night for the next week. He was awakened by the goat-man again on Thursday night, but the visit was brief. The beast merely stated, "Time for you to get a new truck. A nice heavy one."

"Why, Krampus?"

"Oh, so you know my name now."

"Yes, I know your name."

"You need a truck for the performance."

Lying next to Manou's warm body, Ernst wanted to wrap his arms around her in safety but instead stared at the ceiling feeling the red-hot wire that tied his guts to the goat-man's demands.

At breakfast, Ernst told his wife, "I want a new truck."

She looked at him with a familiar curious, somewhat removed expression that annoyed him although he knew how and why it had sprung from her face. She knew about the mess of his mind even if she never admitted it to him—or herself. He had the best tools to deny it and cover it up: absence and arrogance.

"What do you need a truck for? We're not going to build another house are we?"

"What? So you can take it away from me like the last one?"

She sighed. "I didn't take anything away from you. We both agreed this was a better school district for the kids. They are happy here."

He looked away. "I just want a truck. To pull the boat up to the mountains."

Manou shrugged. "Alright. If it makes you happy, buy a truck."

That afternoon he went to the Ford dealer and looked at all the pickup models. He chose a cherry red 1969 F250 Ranger with a 360 V8 engine and a heavy-duty bumper. "To haul our camper and our boat," he told the salesman. It had a crew cab so there was room for the kids.

That weekend, while Manou was skiing at Squaw Valley with Lucy, he took the kids on a road trip in his beautiful new truck. They cruised up to Bodega Dunes north of San Francisco. It was a great day, climbing along the cliffs and hiking through the dunes. He was grateful for them. They were reality. They were solid ground. When they were with him, it cooled the compulsions burning his mind.

About four in the afternoon, mist collected over the beach. They got back in the F250 and headed into the mountains on Highway 1. As the road cut through a canyon, the last sunlight hit the top of the hillside. Out of the corner of his eye, Ernst saw the goat-man skipping through the brush. Ernst gripped the steering wheel so tight his knuckles hurt. Sophia was sitting beside him. He nudged her. "There on the hillside. See the man who has the horns and hooves of a goat?"

"Where, Dad?"

"Up there." He pointed to the line between the canyon shadow and the sun on the hill.

The two in the crew cab peered out the window. Francis answered, "Oh, yes, Dad, I see it, I think. Near the pine tree?"

Karl scoffed in his new low voice, "There are a thousand pine trees up there."

"I see. I do. He's skipping like he's happy." Florence giggled.

"Yes, that's what he's doing." Ernst felt great relief. Maybe the apparition wasn't just a figment of his imagination.

Sophia said, "Come on. There's nothing there."

"Really, he's up there to the left."

"Dad, are you trying to hypnotize us?" asked Sophia, and the kids all laughed.

Ernst drove on, and he understood completely, finally. No one could see the goat-man, talk to the goat-man, or obey the goat-man but himself.

That evening, as Ernst soaked in a warm bath he heard the familiar tapping on the window above the tub. The yellow eyes gleamed in on him. "Practice," mouthed the creature. "Practice."

Ernst slipped under the water and held his breath. Held it. Held it. Held it, until he began to feel the hot throbbing in his chest and the desire to surge upward to release the toxic carbon dioxide in his lungs.

Instead of seeking relief, though, he began the hypnotic count: 100, 99, 98, 97, 96... He could have gone on but he heard the bathroom door open.

Ernst slipped upwards and the water washed away from his face. He released the air slowly from his chest and smiled at his son.

"Dad, are you playing underwater man again?" Francis asked.

"Yes. I'm pretty good at it."

"You're the best," the boy said. Francis leaned over and splashed his father, and then he turned on the faucet at the sink and began to brush his teeth.

When the kids settled down, Ernst went to the bedroom and turned on his flicker light. It had soothed him the first few times he used it but it had become less and less effective. He tried increasing the frequency. He stared at the fast blinking light. Soon crystalline drop-like shapes appeared before his eyes like a kaleidoscope of splattering water. The splatters were soon intruded upon by slashes of red. It was Krampus' tongue. "No. I told you. I am too good to be taken away by a cold river. Go away," ordered Ernst as if disciplining one of his children. He shut off the flicker light, but a voice echoed in his mind. It whispered the words Mutti used when she spanked him with the wooden spoon, "You will do as I say. Bad boy." Ernst made a weak attempt to resist. "I won't," he whispered, but he heard his own weakness and it angered the goat-man.

"You think you can resist? I'll show you."

Ernst crushed his hands over his ears, curled up like a fetus, and rolled away from the light. Suddenly it was quiet. He fell into a long, dark, deep sleep.

The phone rang next morning. "Ernst," Manou called to him from downstairs. "It's someone from the Stanford lab."

Ernst felt groggy but ambled to the phone in the upstairs hall. "Hello, this is Ernst."

"This is Sam."

"Okay."

Silence.

"Sam? What? Do we have subjects to test today? I thought our next session was Wednesday..."

"No. It's not about that. I just...I just thought I should let you know..."

Ernst began to get irritated at Sam's fumbling. "Let me know what?"

"It's Jeremy."

"What about Jeremy?"

"He drowned yesterday."

Ernst was stunned. Ernst also heard Jeremy's voice say, I am a man of mystery, Dr. Feidler. Like you. "What do you mean he drowned? How?"

"He was in a boat alone...fishing, I think... and it capsized or somehow he went overboard without a lifejacket. His body washed up on the shore."

The words of the goat-man rushed back: I'll show you.

Sam continued, "Man, drowning must be a horrible way to die."

Watch what you catch with the Dreammachine. Jeremy had warned him.

"I don't know. Anyway, thanks for telling me."

After Sam hung up, Ernst leaned against the wall trembling. Manou trotted up the stairs but stopped when she saw his face. "Was that bad news?"

He nodded. "Unbelievable. A guy from the hypnosis lab died yesterday."

"I'm so sorry. Was he a friend?"

"Not really. I hardly knew him."

"But you seem so upset by it."

Ernst hesitated, and then he said, "He drowned."

"That's awful. Out of the blue?"

"Yes, awful." But fear made Ernst's ears ring. He understood. It was not out of the blue. It was a message from Krampus: Practice. There was no alternative. Yes, Ernst understood it was almost time for the final performance.

More and more Ernst had inhabited two places at once: a gauzy distant alluring landscape and ordinary earth. He was ashamed of being split. He must hear the clarity of each note and each variation until his performance could be like a sphere, seamless and whole. Now that the choice had been made, the performance would take him to the simpler terrain.

Standing in the hall, straddling the two realms, he watched Manou talking with Sophia, dressing, and shuffling the little atomic particles of their life around the house. She was one of the variations he must release with eloquence. Her sinuous strength and beauty had so often drawn him back to ordinary earth, yet the lovelier and more embodied Manou had become over the years, the more ephemeral he felt. She would be fine without him. She deserved a tender farewell.

Ernst waited all week. At dinner on Thursday, he handed Manou a box of chocolates for Valentine's Day. Her look of shock made him laugh.

"You've never..." she began, and put her hand to her mouth.

Florence exclaimed, "Wow, Dad, that is so sweet. Can I have the cherry-filled one?"

Manou opened the heart-shaped box and passed it around the table. When she got to Ernst, she hugged him tightly and kissed him.

On Sunday morning, he walked up behind Manou and put his arms around her. At first, her body stiffened in surprise, but then she leaned into him and looked over her shoulder with such raw pleasure that it made him catch his breath. "Would you take a drive over to Pleasant Hill with me. I'd like to see the house we built together."

Manou looked at his face. Apparently seeing that he wasn't going to complain again about the move to Walnut Creek, she agreed. They drove up Highway 680 and Ernst turned the red truck into the neighborhood. No one was home. They got out of the car and walked the grounds quietly together. Ernst thought about time as swift, flickering moments that passed so quickly. Like the hypnotic box, at first it was a balm, and then it was frenetic and aggravating.

As they crossed the backyard, he felt like a camera picking out small isolated details: trees, shrubs and flowers they had planted in the yard, flagstone he laid outside the back door, and stones he lined up for terracing. "Look, Manou, the kids used to race to that old sycamore over there." Now they stood on the back deck and stared at Mount Diablo the way they had done countless evenings and weekends. Ernst looked down at a board that had cupped in the weather. He put his arm around Manou's waist. "We hammered every board into place, didn't we?"

"In two houses!" She laughed—a little too loudly—with the spirit he used to find so infectious. "And I was pregnant with Florence when we built the duplex!"

He glanced at her sharply. Was she scolding him for this? No, her face held the wonder of a story that had happened to other people in another time.

They looked over their creation in silence for a while longer. He felt the music of their dance together flow off his wife. But it was not the music he had been practicing. He had to move away from her. "I've seen it. Now we can go," he said, and they got back in the truck.

They stopped at a small café for sandwiches on the way back to Walnut Creek. He sat across from her sipping coffee and eating. Now it was time to free her. He put his sandwich down. "You know that little rat in the maze? Your analysis of us?"

Manou looked hesitant, careful, vulnerable, like she wasn't sure how to react, so she finally just nodded.

"Now I understand what you meant."

"Oh, Ernst." Her cheeks illuminated with a rose-colored blush. "I didn't know you even read that."

He reached across the table and touched her hand. "Manou, you'll see. Everything will be good for you." Feeling a surge from his chest, like he might cry, he smiled across the worn thread that still connected them. It was the smile that he knew had always melted her, as it did now. He could see a soft creamy texture flow under her skin. Her eyes let out a beacon of light, another invitation for him to return to her. He nodded, but not at her false hope. He let her think that, although he really was silently applauding his performance, so nuanced, well paced, and meticulously executed.

Sunday night, as he said goodnight to Karl, Sophia, Florence, and Francis, he bathed each in a secret, nourishing light. They didn't notice, of course, but he saw it enter their blood streams. It would not be easy for them to understand their father's final performance, but this elixir of light would feed them during their plague of grief. It would make them strong.

On Monday morning, he dressed in his best blue suit. As he stood at the dresser, he looked at the pieces of his identity that no longer applied. The blond man on his driver's license. The credit card with his name: Ernst Feidler. The dollar bills and coins that belonged to a country that did not feel like his even after so many years. His leather wallet, flat and worn at the corners, lay on the polished wood surface. It was empty except for a twenty-deutschmark bill he always left folded in a pocket of the billfold, a bill he had brought with him to America almost twenty years earlier. It was a glimpse of his only true identity, but that's all he needed until the end of the day.

Ernst drove to Valley College with the confidence he always felt when he had a grand plan. He felt elated during his first two introductory German classes for freshman. He felt compassion that they had no idea yet how complicated language and life would become, so he fed them entertaining words that kept them laughing. After lunch, he had the German III group. They did grammar well enough but had terrible pronunciation. He began to try a hypnosis technique, explaining, "If you relax, you can let go of your inhibitions. You will hear the German phrasing without the influence of English. Come here, Eric."

He chose a student who was a football player and very popular with the girls. He chose him thinking that if this young man could be hypnotized, the rest would accept the method.

"So, sit here." He pulled a chair to face the class. Eric sat down with a thump, a sarcastic grin on his face.

"Now, close your eyes."

Eric jammed his eyes shut and lifted his arm straight out, saying "Heil, Professor Feidler."

The class snickered. Ernst was shocked at the insolence in the sallow, pimply faces. Didn't they know he was offering them an extraordinary opportunity and that his method was brilliant? "Eric, stop your foolishness. Settle down and relax."

"I vill do vat you say, mein fuehrer."

The class snickered again.

Ernst felt humiliated and crushed by the disrespect that he usually ignored. What was wrong with him? Did they see his weakness? His face burned. He felt dizzy. The florescent lights fluttered. He could not spend another minute in front of these mocking faces and impudent voices. He ran out of the classroom.

Down the hall, he swung open his office door to find the goat-man sitting at his desk. "So you are ready."

Ernst nodded, breathing hard and sweating.

"Have you practiced?"

Ernst nodded, but his heart was an engine racing in his chest.

The goat-man ran a languid hand across his horns. The sensual gesture taunted Ernst. Ernst looked down at his hands. They were trembling. He felt nauseous.

Ernst escaped his office. He stopped briefly at the administration office to tell the secretary he was sick and was going home. He drove the truck south on Highway 680 towards Stanford. This was the plan. Before the exit to Alamo, he passed the embankment where the truck could easily slip into the water. He had stopped here countless times as he drove back and forth to Stanford.

Ernst slammed on the brakes. Coward! he heard the goat-man snicker. "Shut up!" he screamed, and gunned the truck in a U-turn over the meridian back towards the highway to Walnut Creek, his home, his bed, and safety.

Tuesday morning, after a night of no sleep, Ernst gave in. The goat-man rattled the window incessantly. Manou dressed like a whore. The flicker didn't help. The kids didn't care. It rained and rained and rained. There was nothing he could do. He tried to sleep but it was impossible with the rain and clicking fingernails on the window.

Ernst got up and dressed slowly and deliberately in a black suit. He tucked his wallet—still empty except for the twenty-deutschmark bill—in his back pocket. As he turned to go down the stairs, unexpectedly Karl came into his mind. He had a science project due and had asked Ernst if they could make a flicker light together. Ernst gripped the banister. "My son needs me, Krampus!" he hollered to the empty house. "Oh God, who can I call. Who will help?"

He saw the address book on the phone table in the hall. He flipped through it frantically until he saw Komarov, Dimitri. Yes, Dimitri was a good man. He believed in my music. He will help."

Ernst dialed the number. It rang. And rang. And rang. And rang.

"Hello?" Dimitri finally answered.

"Dimitri. I...I need your help."

"Who is this, please?"

"Ernst Feidler."

"Ernst, I didn't recognize your voice. You sound so strange."

Ernst whispered hoarsely into the phone, "I don't know what to do."

"What's wrong, my friend?"

"I'm afraid."

"Of what?"

"I'm dizzy. I can't think. I don't know what to do. I can't face those students again."

"Look," Dimitri said, "it sounds like you might be sick. Do you have a doctor?"

"Yes. Dr. Tremont."

"Well, I think you should call him. He'll help you."

"Yes. Thank you. That's good advice. That's what I'll do." Ernst hung up. He jumped back as the phone rang as soon as he put the receiver in the cradle. He picked it back up automatically.

"Ernst?" It was Manou. He had to get rid of her.

"How are you doing?" she shouted into the phone. He could hear the rain pelting somewhere behind her. Or was it Krampus?

"Okay...I'm doing okay."

"Who called?"

"I was just talking to Dimitri." He couldn't let her suspect. "He's going to watch my classes."

"That's good. I'm glad you're staying home. The weather is terrible, so typical of February. Keep warm."

He had nothing to say to her anymore.

"I wish I could be in bed, too...with you," she said.

The whore.

"I'll be home after my last class. I'll pick up the kids and bring something good for dinner."

"You ought to get back to class. Good-bye."

He had to get rid of her.

He had to protect her.

He had to get rid of her.

He had to protect her.

His mouth was dry as he picked the phone up again and dialed 911. "What is your name and what is your emergency?"

"My name is Ernst Feidler and," his tongue caught in his mouth, "my wife...suicide...my children...please."

"Where is your wife, Mr. Feidler?"

He swallowed and licked his lips. "She is teaching at Contra Costa High School."

"And she is suicidal?"

Ernst felt confused. The dispatcher didn't make sense. His voice caught in his throat again. "Please help."

"We will, sir. Can you give me a number where you can be reached?" But Ernst had already hung up and headed downstairs. His legs trembled. Maybe he really did have the flu. Dimitri said to call Dr. Tremont. He went back to the kitchen and drank a glass of water. Now he could talk again. He picked up the wall phone and called Dr. Tremont's number that was taped to the refrigerator.

"May I speak to Dr. Tremont?" he asked the receptionist.

"He's awfully busy. Can I have him call you back?"

"No!" shouted Ernst, "This is an emergency."

"All right, sir, calm down. Whom shall I say is calling?"

"Ernst Feidler. Professor Ernst Feidler."

In a minute, Dr. Tremont picked up. "What's going on, Ernst?" He sounded a little irritated.

"I don't know. I just can't do it anymore. I think...I think something is terribly wrong."

"Describe to me what you are feeling?"

"Dizzy. Nauseous. I hear...a voice." Ernst began to whisper. "He is coming to take me and I don't want to go. Sometimes I do. But not always."

"Okay, Ernst. I can't see you now because I've got three screaming babies with strep throat or tonsillitis or something in the waiting room. Here's what you need to do. Go over to the emergency room at Kaiser Hospital and ask to see a mental health physician. Do you hear me?"

Ernst stood up straight. Yes, I can do that.

"Ernst, do you hear me?"

"Yes, Dr. Tremont. I'll do that. Right now. Kaiser Hospital."

"Good. Call me when you get home."

"Yes. Goodbye."

Ernst headed for the door. Okay. He had a place to go.

An hour later, Ernst was driving the red truck toward Highway 680 and north to the mental hospital in Martinez. Ernst had told the Kaiser Hospital psychiatrist, Dr. Campbell, everything. About the goat-man. The voice. His plan. His fear. Campbell told him he needed to commit himself to the mental hospital in Martinez for observation. Ernst agreed but he had left the emergency room before the doctor came back with the paperwork. He knew if he waited, he would lose his nerve.

It was pouring rain; the truck shimmied on the road because he was driving too fast. It was a dark, dark gray day, and the headlights of cars coming toward him bounced off the black pavement like the flicker. It hurt his eyes and gave him a headache.

"Ha!" he heard behind him. Ernst's heart sank. He knew that voice as well as he knew his own. "So you are going to be committed to an insane asylum like a blubbering idiot."

"No. It's just for observation. I can't function anymore."

"You are a coward and a failure."

"No! I am sick. The doctor said I was sick. It might be because of my thyroid. Or Sarcoidosis. Or too much Scotch."

"Excuses. You are just a whimpering little hypochondriac. What happened to your pride? Where is your courage?"

Ernst began to cry. "Lost."

"There is a way to get it back."

"No, it's gone, all gone. Like my music."

"You know how to get it back. You've practiced. You have this beautiful, heavy truck. You said goodbye to Manou. We have a plan."

Ernst listed all those pieces in his mind. Practice. Plan. Manou. Pride. Yes. Maybe Krampus was right. He had one last chance to save his dignity.

The entrance ramp for 680 was up ahead. He had entered the highway here so many times to drive south to Stanford. Martinez was north. He took the south loop of the cloverleaf and headed towards his destination; it was like entering his driveway at home. Just past the sign that said ALAMO 2 MILES, Ernst took a deep breath and took his foot off the accelerator. The red truck lost speed slowly. A few impatient cars honked and passed him. He braked and turned onto the shoulder. He wiped his fogged up door window and looked out. There was the water, paralleling the highway, 200 feet below. There was the open embankment.

"Don't get hurt yet," Krampus warned. "That would ruin it all."

"Quiet. I'll do it perfectly," Ernst said out loud, angry, taking over.

"Yes, I'm sure you will," said Krampus, his voice fading back into the patter of rain.

"Five movements. Each part. I've practiced." Ernst asserted, and he turned the wheel sharply and bent down across the passenger seat with his hands on his head so he wouldn't slam it on the windshield. He squeezed his eyes shut, feeling the truck bump down in its 200-foot descent from the freeway, across the concrete shore, and into the water. The first movement, The Dark Dance. Complete.

The truck splashed through the surging water. Soon the drenched engine coughed and ceased, but descent had given the truck momentum. The wheels kept moving through the creek. Water splashed over the hood and past the cab as the truck bumped along on. When it stopped, Ernst sat up, blinked until his eyes saw clearly, and watched the current rush by him. The Running Dance. He had not missed a beat.

The water was filthy brown with silt, but it only went up to the door handle. Ernst lowered the window. He put his feet on the seat and pushed himself through the opening. Holding the edge of the door, he rolled out in a somersault, his back curling over slowly like a gymnast, until he lowered his entire body into the water. Ernst let go of the door and squatted down until the water reached his neck. He took in a long, deep breath. Held it and let it out. Then he took in another, even deeper. Held it. He lowered himself completely underwater. The Slow Dance. Smooth. He felt proud.

Ernst reached down to grab the bottom frame of the truck. He slid himself underneath the vehicle, feet first. He opened his eyes but the muddy water was too opaque for him to see. It didn't matter. Hand over hand, he pulled himself from the bottom of the door, across the now cool exhaust pipe, to the front axle. He wrapped his fingers around the metal bar and held on tight, letting his body bob gently in the flow. The Folk Dance. So simple. Now for the final movement.

Ernst's lungs were burning but he knew how to get through this. First, he thought of his mother. He would never disappoint her now. Then he imagined running with his children on the dunes at Bodega Bay. He was a child, too, light and fast. He next sent his mind to Chilnualna Falls with Manou, and his body felt warm underwater as it had there—and everywhere—with her. Envisioning all of this, he felt exquisite harmony, and he knew he had triumphed over the devil of the Devil's Dance. Ernst smiled and let go.

♫

Once, Dr. Vincent asked Manou to look through the memorabilia of her marriage. She had tried. It was too hard. It was too confusing. Before the fourth anniversary of Ernst's death, though, Mutti asked her for some of the old pictures. Manou finally felt strong enough to rummage through the boxes again and see what she could find for the sad woman who still lived for her son.

Manou brought a carton marked "Photos" down from the attic. She began pulling back the tape, hesitating with fearful respect for the way mementos can spring out of their dust and ashes. She pulled out a folder full of pictures. There were many of Ernst as a child. These were for Mutti so she put them in a large envelope. One picture was of the family, including Mutti, at Lake Shasta. Manou remembered that Ernst had asked the people camping next to them to take the snapshot so the whole family could be in it. They posed around a big campfire roasting marshmallows. She added that to the envelope, too. The next was taken on Francis's birthday a week before Ernst died. He seemed absolutely normal, smiling—oh, that hypnotic smile. She peered at the picture carefully and noticed that Ernst was a little heavy and his eyes did have circles under them. If only she had known what would happen a few days later, what could she have done differently? Nothing. His posture still exuded command of all around him, and she could hear his voice calling the kids together to eat cake and open presents.

Surprising herself, Manou welcomed more memories. She reached in the carton and her fingers hit upon a little metal box. She brought it out from amongst the photos and folders. She opened the lid and inside found a folded twenty-deutschmark bill. It was the one found in Ernst's wallet when he was pulled from the water of Danville Creek. She unfolded it, turned it over, and smoothed it out.

"Why did I keep this?" she mused aloud. "No reason. I'll take it to the bank tomorrow."

She fiddled with the bill without really looking at it. Its inscriptions and drawings melted together in the yellow-green water stains. Manou's perception was already colored by her intention to cash it the next day. It's nothing but a banknote, she thought. But it begged a question: why was it in Ernst's pocket? Why was it the only thing in Ernst's pocket. He had no driver's license, no dollars, no addresses, no pictures, and no credit cards. Nothing but this note. Manou eyes began to focus on the details of the deutschmark to find the answer.

Her heart started to beat very fast. Her ears rang. Her face burned. "I have been so, so blind, she whispered. " It was so obvious, so poignant, and so austere. This was Ernst's true voice. It was his suicide note.

On one side, the bill held the figure of an enigmatic woman with full lips, high cheeks, and sad eyes. Her faraway glance spoke of a great loss. "I know you so well, Mutti," said Manou to the image. "You spent a total of seven years with us, almost half of our sixteen years of marriage. Ernst could never be without you very long. Your devotion was endless. I could never match that piety towards any other human, not even Ernst."

Manou stared at the soft features of a Madonna, the dreamy eyes veiling her obsession. It was the perfect image of Mutti at about thirty, when Ernst was a little boy. An old jealousy rose in Manou. This pretty, sensual woman on the deutschmark was an unassailable ideal implanted in Ernst's mind since infancy. He had looked all his life for a similar virginal creature, self-sacrificing, irreproachable, submissive. He never found her, and he berated Manou regularly for not meeting that expectation. Manou was the flirtatious French girl; she was Marie Madeleine the sinner and prostitute. Myths ruled the psyche and these two myths—that Mutti was pure and Manou was impure—had toppled their love. In the end, Mutti prevailed.

Manou slowly turned the bill over. On the other side was a violin, its bow resting on the strings. "This was the other disappointing love of your life, Ernst. It was the dream abandoned. It was the irredeemable sense of failure."

The mute melancholy of the yellowed deutschmark exposed the repeating themes of Ernst Feidler's life, like the themes of the Partita that rose again and again in each movement. Manou heard the variations of the final passionate Ciaconna that she had listened to over and over in his practice. They were the complex themes of Ernst's lost illusions: the creative sustenance of music, his demand for his own perfection, and the perfection of an idealized woman.

Those around him were an admiring audience to his many successes while he only saw the failures. When he couldn't bear this shame anymore, he left the simplest confession. The images on the deutschmark held the truth.

Manou pressed the bill to her chest. She knew her sorrow for his fate was etched into her flesh like the images on the bill. The inaudible music of his Partita was not written in the score or captured in any performance. It was his spirit. She heard his now distant voice, and she understood it.

Air

The Dance of Lost Illusions

Francis put down Mutti's letter. "Mom, I don't understand why she wants you to come see her after what she said to us." He looked puzzled and a little angry. The whole family was eating lunch by the pool under a soft May sun. Florence and Francis still lived at home. Sophia worked in San Francisco so she came home often. Karl had driven up from UCLA and brought the mail from the box by the driveway, including the letter from Hof.

Manou paused before she answered Francis. The kids had gone to Europe at least once a year in the six years since Ernst died—to see Mutti as well as Maman, Odette, and Marraine. The trips had been exciting for them. They had become good friends with their cousins and come back every year speaking French and German and filled with that indescribable confidence that came from traveling abroad. When Francis and Florence went to see Mutti over last spring break, however, their experience had been deeply disturbing. Florence had casually mentioned that Manou was dating, and Mutti went into a tirade of bitter accusations.

"Her face was so furious," said Florence with a shiver. "And she told us everything that happened to Dad was your fault."

Manou nodded. Mutti had said things that she really had no business saying to her grandchildren.

Manou had seduced Ernst in college.

Manou made him marry her by getting pregnant.

Manou prevented Ernst from returning to Germany.

Max wouldn't have died if Ernst had lived in Hof.

Manou made Ernst quit playing the violin.

"Your mother is a whore," Mutti had said. And more.

Florence tried to describe Mutti's face and voice as she said these things. "I've never seen anyone look that mad. She looked like this," and she furrowed her brow.

"No," said Francis, "like this." He turned down his lips, squinted his eyes, and rasped in German, "*Ihre schreckliche Mutter* ...your horrible mother."

Karl laughed. "She used to get mad at me like that all the time... *schrecklicher Junge*...awful boy."

"She was sweet to me," said Francis.

Sophia added, "That's because you look just like Dad."

"Come on, you guys, she was pretty nice to all of us." Florence paused. "But this time Mutti was just plain mean."

For kids life was all black and white, right and wrong, Manou thought as she listened to them. Adulthood was the frustrating process of recognizing that all behaviors were mazes of nuance, gradations not absolutes.

"Yes, Francis, I'm going to accept her invitation and you know why."

"I know. You said she's lonely. It still didn't give her the right to say those awful things about you."

"It's more than loneliness. I think it is emptiness. She literally has no one. No husband. No family. No children. She feels she has to protect Ernst because he can't speak for himself. It makes her feel connected. We have each other so we can be a little forgiving."

Sophia added, "You also said if we pretended her outburst never happened, she would get over it. I guess she did."

Manou sighed and read the letter again. "So, I'll be off to the Black Forest in June. It should be very pretty."

The two-bedroom cabin Mutti rented for them was a very traditional mountain hideaway. It had a steeply sloped shingle roof, dark wood inside and out, trimmed with hunter green shingles, windowsills, and doors. There were walking trails through the pine forest and cows that grazed right up to the windows.

Unfortunately, it rained every day. Mutti had always been a quiet person so their conversation was slim. Mutti looked at her askance every once in while as if waiting for Manou to say something. Manou assumed she was concerned about her accusations to the kids and might even be embarrassed. Manou was glad she had let it go.

Mutti didn't want to go out much because of the weather and because her legs were swollen from the medicine she was taking for her heart. Mutti seemed fragile to Manou, the former coolness and distance now seemed more like shyness. Manou contented herself with making meals for her and sharing the one activity they had in common: knitting. Manou sat in the dimly lit sitting room of the cabin across from her mother-in-law and allowed herself the simple companionability this vacation offered them. She felt the two of them were connected to the communion of women over history who knitted or sewed or did needle point together. They didn't need to talk much, as if the rhythm of their fingers was a silent meditation on life.

Nonetheless, after four days, Manou started getting restless. Mutti was napping in her own room that afternoon so Manou paced around the small space and then gazed out the window, longing to hike on the paths through the forest. But rain pelted the earth and she felt stuck. She leaned on the sill and something pinched her elbow. It was Mutti's wedding ring. Her mother-in-law had taken it off because her fingers were a little swollen, too. Manou picked it up and twirled it in her fingers. She noticed the inscription inside the band: Max und Marie, November 1929. November? But Ernst was born in December 1929. Manou chuckled. Mutti was eight months pregnant when she married Max. Pregnant! Ernst's saintly mother was no virgin when she married. What?

At first, this information seemed merely amusing to Manou; in the next moment, it had the impact of a revelation. She felt an irresistible laughter rumble to her throat and she had to run before she exploded with elation. She burst out the door of the cabin and raced through the rain into the forest. She ran and ran, screaming, letting Mutti's perfection tumble from its pedestal and scatter across the wet pine needles. Away from the cabin, laughter burst from her guts and she roared as she ran. What unbelievable irony. Ernst's harsh judgment about Manou, that she still held inside every time she tried to get involved with someone new, was based on an utterly false comparison to his supposedly virtuous mother. The myth had collapsed—if only for Manou—but she savored this tender knowledge of humans' effort to hide their shame under cover of righteousness and perfection. Manou sprinted along the alpine path breaking out of her unaware past into an awakened future. In this delicious dance of lost illusions, Manou rushed down the trail like a little girl in the hills of La Bâtie, her heart flooding with joy.

As dusk approached, Manou walked back to the cabin breathing deeply, drenched in summer rain. She felt physically spent, liberated, at peace, cleansed of the burden of guilt. Mutti came out of her bedroom, took one look at Manou's wet clothes, and exclaimed, "Manou, dear, what is wrong?"

Manou shrugged with a silly grin on her face. How could she explain that now everything was just right?

Mutti grabbed a towel and began drying her daughter-in-law with the gruff attention she paid to those she loved. With her swollen fingers, Mutti tried to rub the rainwater off Manou's wet sweater. Manou felt a rush of kindness for the woman she now had known longer than Ernst. Manou hugged her quickly and quietly, to Mutti's surprise. Manou would never try to explain to Mutti the complicated, sad man who was her son, and she would never tell her that he had committed suicide. It would break the fragile heart that still held up her aging body.

Manou could not absorb the full impact of her new understanding of the Feidler family until she returned home to her quiet room, her sanctuary, the place where she had met her own madness and her peace. When she had a moment alone after greeting the kids, Manou turned on the music that had saved her sanity: Air on a G String by Bach. It's throbbing heartbeat and soothing passages embraced the tragedy that had so deeply affected her life. She looked out at Mount Diablo as Ernst had done the day he ended his own life, and her elation was replaced by a sudden melancholy about human nature. Unacknowledged shame had wracked her husband's spirit. Family secrets manipulated lives for generations. Where would she be today if Ernst had not ended his life? Would they still be fighting their neurotic battles? Would he have continued drinking? Would his desperation ever have abated? Would he have rediscovered his music and his hope? His death had been a rebirth for her, she knew. Perhaps that is what he meant when he had told her, "Manou, you'll see. Everything will be good for you." All right, yes, but at what a devastating cost.

What revealed secrets before they destroyed a life? In her case, revelation occurred through two accidental discoveries: the suicide note encoded in the images on a deutschmark and a marriage date inscribed on the inside of a ring. She now desperately wanted to find a more intentional way to expose and purge the poison of secret guilt, especially for her children, who would have to deal with the tragedy of their father's death, each one in his and her own way. It would not be easy. It might take her lifetime and theirs, but they would look forward not back.

The peaceful yet strong melody of the Air filled the room with hope. The violin evoked the best she had shared with Ernst as they first headed west together: when they looked toward the future, they were one and invincible.

Endnotes

Air on the G String

A melody which grows always more eloquent as one listens, not only because of its noble beauty, but also because of its wisdom, the tenderness, the profound knowledge of life which speak from every measure.

Olin Downes, The Lure of Music: Picturing the Human Side of Great Composers, with Stories of Their Inspired Creations, Harper & brothers, 1922, page 12.

Partita for Violin No. 2

The Partita in D minor for solo violin (BWV 1004) by Johann Sebastian Bach was written between 1717–1723, and some scholars suggest it was written in memory of Bach's first wife, Maria Barbara Bach. The Partita contains five movements:

Allemanda

Corrente

Sarabanda

Giga

Ciaccona

A strong common theme is shared between the first four movements. In the Allemanda, there is a hint at the repeated bass, which from then on haunts the piece until it makes its full appearance in the Ciaconna. While the first four movements reflect the standard German baroque dance suite, the overall dark character of the Partita is enhanced by the monumental Ciaccona, which closes the work.

Krampus

According to various Alpine European traditions, St. Nicholas visited children on the eve of December 5. Chained to him was an evil, goat-horned spirit named Krampus. The word Krampus originates from the Old High German word for claw ("Krampen"). While St. Nick was a gentle benefactor bringing gifts and candy to children, Krampus brought switches and bad dreams to naughty boys and girls. The character stemmed from the pagan practices of ancient Europe in which he was a trickster with long shaggy fur, big horns, cloven hooves, and a long red tongue. He was chained to St. Nick so he was under control. Otherwise, he might beat little children or, as happened in some traditions, lure them into the woods to eat them.

About the Author

Madeleine Herrmann was born in Lyon, France, on March 17, 1930. She lived through the World War II years in Nantes, which was bombed repeatedly by the Americans.

After the war, Madeleine became a competitive athlete who won French national track and field titles and participated in the University World Games in 1949 in Budapest. She studied in Paris for two years at the Ecole Normale Supérieure d'Éducation Physique then received a Fullbright scholarship to study at the University of Iowa. There she met Fred Herrmann, a German linguist and gifted violinist.

Madeleine and Fred defied the age-old hostility between the Germans and the French and married. They lived in California, built two houses, and raised four children. Madeleine pioneered physical fitness classes for women and children in California and graduated from UC Berkeley in 1962 with a master's degree. She taught French at Del Valle High School, then at Diablo Valley College in Pleasant Hill, California. Fred Herrmann committed suicide in 1969.

In 1983, Madeleine went back to college to study Transpersonal Psychology in the master's program at JFK University in Orinda, CA. She has lived in Taos, New Mexico, since 1992.

In 1986, her book of poetry, *L'Envolée Magique* (Editions Saint-Germain-Des Prés), was published in France. In it she explored "the essence of the feminine and the masculine." She has continued writing poetry, plays, short stories, a children's story, and this psychological novel, exploring the mysteries of human sorrow, love, and music.

PO Box 3223. Taos, NM 87571
madeleineherrmann@msn.com
575-751-1051